THE

TROLL

by Brian Darr

Library of Congress Control Number: 1-2453982391

ISBN-13: 978-1511407205

ISBN-10: 1511407204

10 9 8 7 6 5 4 3 2 1

First Edition United States

This book would not have been possible without my step-daughter, who inspired me to write a story that she might like. Thanks for reminding me how to be young.

-To Iris-

PART I

CHAPTER 1

The only faces of what little revolution was left belonged to The Surfer and Wigeon. In fact, they were probably the only two people left on the planet that cared at all. Word was they had a small gathering of people who worked behind the scenes, but even if that were true, their belief that the world could ever be restored was laughable to everyone else.

No one really cared that the world was taken over anymore. They did at first, but after awhile, the population got used to how things were and adjusted. Everyone is afraid of the apocalyptic scenario: The world rips apart and falls into complete anarchy and the underdogs have to battle the hostile primitive evils that conquered. When the world came to an end, it was soon discovered that the new version wasn't so bad.

The new world was pretty simple. All complex and useful things that man made were suddenly gone. There were no longer vehicles, weapons, phones; Even electricity was scarce. Twenty years ago, anyone reading this would have said "no way Jose. Couldn't deal with that," but before all those things existed, people got by just fine, and when those things were gone, they figured out how to function, and in some ways, better than before.

The Surfer and Wigeon never recovered from the fall though. They could never forget the intentions of the guys who ran things and all the casualties in the beginning. No one disagreed that their takeover wasn't just a greedy power move, but what they did was intelligent and a lot of people believed that the world actually improved when it got simpler—even with great sacrifice.

No weapons were used in the takeover. There was no militia, bombs, blackmail or threats. It was just a group of guys who worked for a company called "Circular Prime Technologies".

A circular prime is a prime number that when the numbers rearrange, is still a prime number, an example being 1931, which can be reconfigured as 9311, or 3119 or any other combination and remain prime. It symbolized the idea that everything is built from things that already exist—that every new invention and idea is a rearrangement of what we already have.

What Circular Prime specialized in was the advancement of cellular technologies. The generation before had only heard of rotary phones, which had advanced into hand-held phones, and then the cell phones with the apps and games. Eventually, no one used phones for their intended purpose. Instead, it was all about organizing life and connecting without really connecting. The powers that be at Circular Prime were the first to launch what had been inevitable, but until it hit the market, had only been talked about as an experiment: The Fibonacci Drive, which was nicknamed simply: Psi.

Psi was a mind-blowing piece of technology. To purchase Psi meant having a quick procedure done, tantamount to getting your ear pierced. You walk into any retail store's Pharmacy and for nearly $400.00, you could have Psi injected right into your brain, and voila! You were connected to the Web. Navigating websites was as simple as thinking about them. Suddenly, a world of information was in the heads of anyone who purchased Psi. It was the tiniest microchip— not visible to the naked eye—embedded in plasma and placed right into people's brains. Texting, tweeting, social networking, and blogging were all done by arranging sequences using only thoughts. It was so awesome at the time, it was scary. Movie plots of robots forming personalities and taking over were suddenly very real threats, but nothing like that happened. Robots didn't do a damn thing. It was people.

The people at Circular Prime who built Psi, to be exact.

No one knew if it was a long planned attack or if they just became disgruntled, but someone in the company had an idea in their head and a small band of followers, and one warm June evening, the whole world changed with the push of a button and about a dozen guys at the controls.

By then, Psi had gotten cheap to inject and it was as much a necessity as cell phones were before that. You'd be hard pressed to find someone without Psi, but there were some who saw the dangers of technology so advanced. The Surfer and Wigeon were good examples of that. The fact was, on that June evening, to NOT have Psi meant being the rare individual who would not be enslaved by this small group of hackers.

For them, it was simple. Everyone had a microchip in their brain and they used it to control the net. Why couldn't they tap into the mainframe and turn Psi around on the users? That's what they ultimately decided to do.

The main developer, a man named Michael Hogan, refused to pack a box and avoid letting the door hit him on the way out. Now, Michael goes by The Moderator, a nickname he basically gave himself. The Moderator and his entourage of hackers and crackers shut down the whole system and rebooted with different coding. When they did this, everyone with Psi shut down for two minutes, aware of their surroundings but unable to respond or react. Millions of people died—people in cars or planes or out for a swim or climbing trees. Everyone was shut down for two minutes and when the system rebooted, chaos broke out. It didn't last long. It lasted as long as it took to realize that someone else had control over the population and could murder any one of us at any moment by typing in an individual identification number and frying the circuit. That would result in something like a stroke, and then a paralyzed state. They were allowed to mourn, but revenge was prohibited and anytime a group of people huddled together to start plotting against the folks led by The Moderator, the leader of the group would suddenly wind up dead. Soon, people got the message and submitting became the only way to survive.

A couple years later, though everyone had lost loved ones, the world became peaceful and sensible. There was no threat of war, no hate crimes, homicides, or anything that ruined lives. The Moderator and his men swept in and confiscated everything. Guns, vehicles, communication devices: All destroyed. The Moderator said it was time to prioritize—that these luxuries should have never been so widespread. People had become lazy and entitled. The world had been made too easy. So he took it all away and it was suddenly primitive again.

Tribes formed and soon hunting, fishing, and gardening were the main source of sustenance. Everything became simple and people learned to work together again without having to text, and that life worked for many. Those who couldn't adapt but who complied by the rules, people who made up a good sized chunk of the population, were still allowed to use computers, but not for information. They worked in large warehouses where the extent of their time at the keyboard was spent on message boards, chatting with others like them.

Everyone either contributed, or stayed out of the way without qualms. There were a lot of rules that if broken, The Moderator would catch onto and shut a person down without thinking twice.

Every now and then, someone would get it in their head to rebel or play against the rules, but since The Moderator knew where everyone was at all times and could communicate with anyone through Psi, he'd warn the individual breaking the rule, and if they continued, their life was cut short. A couple years ago, there was a sort of mass suicide when a group of people got together and tried to storm Circular Prime. They didn't even get within a mile of the city before they were all dead.

Circular Prime was built in what was once Chicago, which is one of the few cities left with any activity. It housed everything that kept the world running. Every connection ran through that area from one of the tallest buildings in the city. No one was allowed to enter the city, which was rumored to be a sort of paradise for those few men. Chicago kept canned foods and TV dinners coming from the city too. The Moderator ate much better than everyone else did, but he also made sure no one starved and he didn't provoke trouble—he only punished those who caused it. It was easy to make people share because the monetary system was extinguished completely. The only value that existed came from individual contributions.

And it kept the world peaceful.

The very minimal revolution of The Surfer and Wigeon was a small exception to that rule, and since they were a few of the only people who didn't have Psi in their heads, they had been fugitives for a long time. They were envied for having the unique distinction of not having to fear being zapped. Still, their cause wasn't taken all too seriously.

Most of the males of the world viewed Wigeon as just a poster girl—a fantasy—and boy did they fantasize about her. When a man decided to join the rebels, it was usually because she recruited them and they wanted her. She was an absolutely beautiful Amazonian, tall, clear eyed, flowing dark haired, full lipped woman. She was most definitely a looker and her capture and death were so tragically inevitable that people tried to pretend like she was a figment of their imagination.

Wigeon was hard to avoid, with posters and sightings and every now and then, The Surfer and Wigeon would hack into the airwaves for a minute or two and try to recruit people into an uprising—which never worked—but holy cow the men in the world went crazy for her. She would always be sporting a tight shirt and flaunting cleavage. Maybe that was part of their marketing plan, and maybe people did join them for that reason, but she was nothing more than a fantasy for most, because to join them and be caught, meant death. Many were caught because some with Psi tried to join up and led The Moderator right to the rebels. Wigeon, while she was the personification of the perfect woman, was unobtainable.

The Surfer had a similar story. He somehow managed to look well-groomed but primitive at the same time. He had the build of a man who climbed and swam and jumped everything in his path, but with a clean shaved face and shapely jaw on his chiseled face. Sometimes people wondered if they really were in charge of a revolution, or if they were placed there as eye candy.

The Surfer and Wigeon didn't successfully rally the people, and so their revolution remained small and inevitably on the path to oblivion, but they lasted longer than expected, and on the day they were caught, a lot of people felt something they didn't think they would: Sadness.

The broadcast and air waves were controlled by The Moderator. The only broadcast towers remaining all were controlled by Circular Prime, but there were towers all over the land so if they had something to say, they transmitted and the screens were impossible to avoid. During a broadcast, you could look into the sky and see hundreds of screens projecting the image of the Moderator. When The Moderator had something to say, everyone saw it. Other than that, TV was just another thing of the past. Every now and then, a rebel would be caught and they would broadcast the trial and execution for all to see, which served as reminders not to go against the men in Circular Prime. The last thing anyone wanted was to be publicly captured and murdered on TV, but that was the fate of refusing to accept reality.

And so they did. At first, by force. Eventually, because it was all they knew. In the course of a decade, most forgot the day everyone blacked out for two minutes. Relatives were no longer mourned and history was only word of mouth without the emotional attachment.

No one knew what The Moderator did with Wigeon. She disappeared from the news stories. Instead, the story became the upcoming trial of The Surfer. They publicized the trial aggressively and encouraged all to watch. Everyone already knew what the outcome would be: Like all rebels before him, he would be executed for everyone to see, but they'd make a fool of him first. When he was gone, one of the last symbols of the world pre-Psi would disappear forever.

CHAPTER 2

What little remained of the revolution numbered in the hundreds. With the population so disconnected, there could be multiple groups of people who didn't carry Psi, but these groups would have no way of finding each other.

Surfer and Wigeon belonged to a group outside of Chicago, which was dangerously close to The Moderator, but necessary for when the day came that a plan had to be carried out.

They holed up in what was once an elementary school that was long abandoned. They maintained the outside of the building to look unoccupied, covering the grounds with weeds and dirt. On the inside, they'd scattered broken glass and other alarm systems to alert those inside of anyone's presence. In the center of the school was a gymnasium where they met on occasion, but mostly they'd grouped into their own families and stayed in the classrooms together, living life in seclusion until the day their leader needed them.

That day hadn't come in a dozen years. Initially, those who joined believed they would be a sort of army that would stomp into Chicago and fight until The Moderator fell and they could remove Psi from the people. There had never been much organization, but what they never fully understood was that The Surfer and Wigeon HAD worked hard to find an attack strategy, but there had never been much optimism in their position.

In the beginning, The Surfer didn't have many leaders in the group. He needed a candidate that could train to be strong and lead an army. What he found was a man who he named The Guide. The Guide wanted to be something more: The Assassin or The Eliminator, but The Surfer told him that to be victorious, he needed to be a good leader, and to have a leader label.

The Guide trained and became strong, as he promised he would, and soon, he was the ultimate warrior. He was a fighter and he taught others to fight. On the battlefield, he could lead any group to a fight, but he wasn't an expert tactician. The Surfer hoped he would be, but he never quiet picked up on the strategic art of war. Instead, he was a soldier, and perfect as a soldier in every way.

The days began to blend together. He constantly waited for The Surfer and Wigeon to come to him with the ultimate plan, but they usually met privately and discussed strategy, though he suspected they never made any progress. It seemed the guys running the world from Chicago had a fairly solid advantage that didn't leave room to be conquered. The Guide waited for his moment, assuming it would ever come, building the resistance from his end while wondering if they would ever even be called on.

Their army was about 75 people strong, which was a weak army when going into a city blind—a city designed to keep people out. Even without Psi, they wouldn't even come face to face with The Moderator. He had too many fancy gadgets, booby traps, and bounty hunters with special abilities of their own. The need for an army became a second thought, which had become more apparent as The Surfer and Wigeon conducted more closed-door meetings.

Then, one day while The Guide was training, a friend delivered the message: The Surfer and Wigeon were captured trying to get into Chicago. Apparently Wigeon had intel that provided a way in without being detected, but the mission backfired and both were taken.

The Guide was a mix of emotions. He was sad that his friends were captured and knew they would be put on trial and killed, but he couldn't help but feel angry too. His set of skills would have been beneficial to their mission, but they hadn't even told him they were leaving. He didn't even get to say goodbye.

Instead of reacting or calling a meeting, he trained harder, until he cramped up and could no longer breath. He threw up, and then trained until he threw up again. The second time, he stayed in the bathroom, heaving over the sink and catching himself in the mirror. It was then that he forced himself to accept a harsh reality: The resistance no longer existed.

When The Guide entered the arena and scanned the crowd, he released a breath of defeat. There were maybe two hundred people remaining, half of their group before The Surfer and Wigeon were caught. He'd expected a drop, but nothing this drastic. Without their leaders, there wasn't much hope left. The torch was passed to The Guide and apparently, no one had faith in that fact.

Joey Dakota was a cab driver before the day of the takeover. His life was boring, without purpose, heading nowhere, but he was content. He was old fashioned, and therefore couldn't care less when Psi rolled out and never had it implanted. After the takeover, he could no longer drive his cab, most of the people he knew were dead, and his lack of purpose was suddenly very real.

When The Surfer hacked into the television for the first time and told everyone to rise up against The Moderator and his gang, The Guide joined because he had nothing better to do and he was one of a small population immune to the power The Moderator held. They came together and The Guide quickly proved himself an expert tactician and became Surfer's friend and adviser. They had been close, but now his friend was captured, and very likely soon to be dead.

He looked up at a large television screen which would ordinarily have been off. Instead, it had a countdown: FIVE MINUTES UNTIL THE TRIAL OF THE SURFER.

The Guide didn't want to watch. He wanted to go back a day in time and tell The Surfer that whatever he was planning, to call it off. He should have seen that they were planning something. They'd spent too much time alone not to. He didn't question his leader, because his leader was the most inspiration anyone had seen in a long time. Their army never grew much. In fact, it shrank, but there were always plans in motion, and The Guide had always believed that one day, The Surfer would find the plan that would beat The Moderator. In hindsight, it seemed foolish. They never had the advantage. They never had an edge. They never even had a chance.

He turned to address the crowd, which was made up of mostly children. "I think maybe the best thing we can do..." The Guide said,

"...is leave the room. I'm not sure we should watch."

"What if he's not convicted?" A voice shouted from the crowd.

"He will be. When was the last time someone was caught and didn't get executed? And it's The Surfer. They consider him to be a bigger criminal than anyone."

"So what? We just let this happen?"

"How do we stop it?"

"Well, you're in charge now, aren't ya?" Someone else asked.

"Surfer was the end of the line for us."

"Well, what the hell are we supposed to do? We can't go home!"

"We never had a chance and we all knew it. What are we supposed to do now? We hadn't persuaded people before and we're sure not going to now...especially now. Everyone in the world just saw the two faces of all that remained of the revolution, get caught. Soon, they'll see them executed. Who in the hell is going to care if a new face surfaces and why in the hell would they follow?"

"Why can't we just start again? We can regroup, rethink our strategy. We can lay low awhile and strike when no one expects it. We don't need to recruit through the airwaves. We can do it on foot."

"Everyone and their brother has Psi people!" The Guide shouted. "We're all that remains and look at us! I've wasted too much time hoping, even when I shouldn't have. We are small. It's time to move on, find a place where maybe we can live our lives without being noticed."

"They'll find us and execute us too," someone shouted. "We have nowhere to go."

"Not every piece of land is monitored. I'm not sure they even know we exist. They've been after Surfer and Wigeon. With them gone, no one will be hunting us." The Guide wanted to let tears fall from his eyes but he held strong. He looked up at the screen: 3 MINUTES UNTIL THE TRIAL OF THE SURFER.

Those bastards in Chicago were probably popping the cork on the champagne already. They caught the remaining representations of life before Psi wiped everyone's brain. They would hold a final demonstration that made the statement: Never go against us.

Everyone waited silently, half watching The Guide and half waiting for the trial that would put an end to it all.

"Look," The Guide started. "If anyone has any ideas of how to get on track, I'm all ears. I get that we're fighting on principle, but we've fought the good fight, much longer than we should have, and that's enough for me. Whatever is waiting for us in our next life, The Moderator will have to face. You were all brave, but when Surfer is dead, no one will be able to stand in his place and have the impact he had. And judging by the population in this room...that was very little."

Their silence was the biggest statement of all. It was agreement. Everything they had worked for was wasted time. Those who tried to take a stand and prove wrong those who believed they couldn't take the world back...they'd been made fools of.

1 MINUTE UNTIL THE TRIAL OF THE SURFER...

One by one, all eyes faced the screen.

When no one was looking, a tear finally fell from The Guide's eyes. He watched and waited.

CHAPTER 3

The Moderator looked up over his glasses and watched the mock courtroom fill with friends and associates. He wore an ash suit, a yellow tie, and his black hair was slicked back with a few strands hanging down. He drank coffee like it was water and his neck twitched uncontrollably from time to time, giving his whole head a jerk. He was always wired and rarely slept. His four o'clock shadow complimented his dark features but his sunken eyes revealed his true age.

He leaned forward in his chair and watched as The Surfer was escorted into court by a tall man who looked like a vampire without the sharp teeth, appropriately named The Mortician. At his side was a shorter wiry man named The Acrobat, whose head was shaved nearly to the scalp. The Surfer held himself together on the outside, but The Moderator knew he was a mess internally. He was trying desperately not to show a sign of weakness, but there was frustration in his eyes as he tugged at his restraints. The Moderator fixated his wide eyes on his enemy.

The cameras began rolling and all over the world, the first trial in over three months began. No one could look away. The Moderator sat back and watched as a strikingly good looking man moved in a liquid motion across the room and approached The Surfer. The man assigned to do the questioning was The Moderator's right hand man. The Magician was a wild card—he constantly had a smile plastered to his face and owned the room with a smug sense of entitlement, but he earned it in what he said.

"Please state your name," The Magician said as a pen smoothly rolled over his knuckles and back to the palm of his hand, doing circles around his hand.

"I go by Surfer."

"What is a Surfer? You surf?"

"At one time, I spent a lot of time browsing on what was known as the World Wide Web."

"Oh, it still is," the Magician said with a laugh. "I always assumed you were named for the act of surfing waves."

"I'm afraid not."

"One would think that the man who was leading a revolution would be more of the surfing waves type and less of a nerd."

"I was cast into this position because my understanding of technology was the very reason I saw the negative impacts in Psi before it shut everyone down."

"Psi was well-intentioned," the Magician shot back and turned to the cameras with a smile. He was showing off for the world to see. He was prepared to make a fool of Surfer.

"Psi may have been well-intentioned at inception, but unfortunately, its potential was harvested by terrorists. I don't blame Psi for what you did anymore than I blame gas instead of Hitler for the systematic execution of millions of people."

The Magician let loose a laugh but he wasn't mocking Surfer. He was genuinely laughing as if he appreciated the reference. He finally caught his breath and focused his attention back to Surfer. "You were caught on the outskirts of Chicago, trying to break into the city with your partner who is known as Wigeon. Please explain to the court what you were doing."

"You know what I was doing."

"Please tell the court."

"Why do you go through these formalities as if they mean something? Why not put a bullet in my head now and stop wasting everyone's time?"

"Everyone is given a chance."

"I'm confused as to how you hold the world hostage and say we have a chance at the same time."

"Please answer the question," Magician said with a pleasant grin.

"In Vegas, there is a secured building which houses a fail safe: A portal which can shut Psi down."

"Then why were you in Chicago?"

"To take the Rainbow from you."

"What is the Rainbow?"

"The thing that appears after a storm," The Surfer said, sarcastically.

Suddenly, the Magician's smile faded and his face became distorted in rage that lasted seconds as he thrust his hands forward and an explosion of blinding fire and dust cracked in front of Surfer's face. The Surfer's eyes went wide and he almost toppled in his seat as the courtroom roared with laughter. He was being made a fool of on a whole new level: Insults and tricks and pointless games before they tossed him from the top of the building…it was all designed to scare the daylights out of anyone with similar aspirations.

When the smoke cleared, the Magician's face was plastered with his friendly smile and he leaned against the witness box awaiting an answer.

The Surfer rubbed his eyes and wheezed. They waited as his breath came back and the Magician calmly asked again. "What is Rainbow?"

"It's just a memory stick."

"And what does it do?"

"If what I've heard is true, plugging it into the system in Vegas means Psi will be overridden everywhere. It means people can be free."

Before the Magician could answer, the Moderator was on his feet, speaking for the first time. "Who says they're not free?"

Everyone's heads turned and the room went quiet. The Magician stood back as The Moderator approached.

The Surfer turned with a smile, happy to address the man he really wanted to spar with. "Taking something by force means enslaving it."

"We cleaned up the streets," the Moderator said. The court nodded and muttered in agreement, if only because it was their leader speaking. "What was the world before? Some utopia? I watched the news Surfer. It was story after story of murder and dirty politics and crime. All that…gone with the stroke of a key. Many many people died, and if I could have fixed things another way, I would have."

"Many people see it differently, and those of us who do, fight to change the world back to how it was before Psi."

"I don't get it," Moderator said. "What was the point of the fight? Surely you don't believe there was ever a way you'd actually get the Rainbow."

"All opinions fall between the fuzzy borderlands of unquestionably true and unmistakably false, and you don't know what we're capable of. You don't care what's best for the world. You were just a nerd, watching TV instead of going on hikes with friends, drooling over porn instead of making love to a beautiful woman. Your greedy mental state steeped you in electronic media and you found your wealth without any time to reflect on what you were doing. You acted on anxiety, rapid emotional swings from euphoria and boredom and frustration that threatened to tip into despair. And all the while, having this unshakable conviction that happiness was around the corner, as soon as you found some semblance of importance or the next raise came along or the delivery guy delivered the Bow-flex you never used. But you found comfort on-line—a bunch of angry geeks like yourself. Put enough people like you together and get them sharing the intimate details of their disease and what you have is a recipe for a revolution that would only strengthen the weaklings. No one denies it was clever, but it wasn't right. Don't try to convince me you believe it was right."

"You got me Surfer. I just wanted a juicy steak to come home to every night, except I believe it was Charles Darwin who once said: How could a selfless individual ever live long enough to reproduce? Why would natural selection favor a behavior that made us less likely to survive? He who was ready to sacrifice his life, as many a savage has been, rather than betray his comrades, would often leave no offspring to inherit his noble nature."

"Darwin also knew altruism was everywhere. It's a stubborn anomaly of nature. Bats feed their own when they're hungry, honeybees commit suicide with a sting to defend the hive, birds raise offspring that aren't their own, humans leap onto subway tracks to save strangers. Goodness is not a losing life strategy."

"I love this, you and I talking," Moderator shot back quickly. "You never stood a chance, but you're at least the closest thing I've ever had to a rival. Everyone else is on a leash, and even though I hate those of you who run around without the chip in you, I'd be lying if I told you I didn't enjoy the chase."

"You'd enjoy it more with a fair fight on a level playing field."

"I once took over the world with a dozen people. I don't think I need to prove to you that I can defy the odds."

"Maybe no one saw it coming because no one expected anyone to do something so shitty."

The Moderator ignored the remark and scratched his head instead. His neck twitched and he suddenly looked up and spoke fast. "I was a pioneer before this, you know that? The good jobs were in programming and I was good. I was really damn good. I worked for Circular Prime, where they manufactured the chips. I started on an assembly line and soon, I was tweaking the design to perfection. I quadrupled the speed. They were forced to dial back on their customer service department because no one complained. Our consumers had the chip inserted and data would upload because their brain wanted it to. They blogged with their minds, had access to anything they wanted, instruction guides, gaming, porn, you name it. They were able to control their own network using their brains, and I was the guy who perfected the process. Back then, I had no dreams of domination. That's for certain. Now, you want to believe I'm just an evil guy who had world domination on my mind, but life was dandy as was. I made good money, loved my work, loved the attention it got me, the prestige that success had to offer, the booze… my goodness I had some good times in the clubs night after night and I wore a new suit every day. I would have done that forever, but the powers that be patented a similar, but lesser quality, Psi. When I objected, what do you know? Goodbye day-job. Hello unemployment line."

"What does that have to do with everyone else?"

"Nothing. What does everyone else have to do with progress? Nothing. You were all just fine test piloting your couches, but unfortunately, when gods fight, they step on insects."

"I already know what happened to you."

"I have a hard time believing many men in my position would have acted differently. In those times, everyone was disposable. They'd say to pack a box and don't let the door hit you on the way out and we all wanted to believe that it couldn't be business as usual without us there, but it was never true. Then, they ousted the wrong man."

"So you became a terrorist."

"I don't see it that way. The difference between living in the city with us and being a part of the rest of the world is tantamount to being a house-pet versus an animal in the wild. Which is really worse?"

"What are you going to do with me?" Surfer finally asked.

"Let's do something different," The Moderator said with a sudden smile, as if a light-bulb lit up over his head. "You and I have been chasing each other for awhile. You're special Surfer. We could debate the pros and cons of Psi all day, but since you believe the world is better off without and I believe the opposite, maybe we let the people decide."

"You'll track and kill anyone that votes my way. How is this a fair resolution?"

"Turn on the monitor," The Moderator said, and suddenly, one wall of the court was a giant computer screen with a flashing dash. "Those of you watching, trust that your honest opinion will not be punished today. I simply want you to tell me what we should do with The Surfer. Should we inject him with Psi and release him? Should we execute him? Today, because The Surfer is special, I will allow him more leverage than I've given in the past."

The Magician started an applause and most of the court followed. When the applause died down and silence filled the room, they turned to the screen.

"Go ahead," The Moderator said. "I know you're all watching."

The dash flashed and everything fell silent.

"Does anyone believe I should show The Surfer mercy?"

It flashed.

"You see that?" The Surfer said. "They're afraid of you. They comply because they are afraid to tell you the truth: The world is better without Psi."

The Moderator's neck twitched and his jaw clenched. He waited another moment and turned back to the court. "I guess this means I make the verdict."

Then, a single ding sounded throughout the court and everyone looked up.

The user-name was Iris and the message wasn't a verdict. It read as a challenge: GIVE THE RAINBOW TO THE PEOPLE. THEY WILL EITHER GIVE IT BACK OR ELIMINATE PSI. YOU WILL

HAVE YOUR ANSWER...

The Moderator's forehead wrinkled and he raised an eyebrow. "What do you mean by that Iris?" he said, looking up toward the camera.

IRIS—YOU CLAIM SURFER NEVER HAD A CHANCE TO TAKE THE RAINBOW AND BEAT YOU. YOU ALSO CLAIM WE WANT PSI...WHY IS THE RAINBOW SO GUARDED IF YOU BELIEVE PSI SHOULD LIVE ON?

"We guard it from terrorists like The Surfer!" The Moderator shouted into the air.

IRIS—IF YOU BELIEVE WHAT YOU SAY, YOU WILL GIVE US A CHANCE TO TAKE THE WORLD BACK.

The Moderator turned to a morbidly obese man named The Weatherman. "Trace this," he said.

As if answering the question for him, the screen dinged and he read: IRIS—I DON'T HAVE PSI.

The Moderator laughed nervously as The Weatherman ran off to find out who the mystery user was. He turned to The Surfer, who seemed equally as confused, but whose eyes were filled with hope. He turned back to the screen. "Who are you Iris?"

IRIS—PART OF THE RESISTANCE. WE'RE LARGER IN NUMBER THAN YOU THINK AND WE HAVE RESOURCES YOU WOULDN'T BELIEVE. WEAPONS, VEHICLES, A DEVICE THAT CAN EXTRACT PSI FROM THE BRAIN...

"What is it you want?"

IRIS—GIVE THE RAINBOW TO THE PEOPLE.

"That won't happen."

IRIS—FROM YOUR FORTRESS, YOU'RE STILL AFRAID. YOU ARE A COWARD BEHIND A BUTTON.

The Weatherman returned, wiping sweat from his forehead. "It's true. The user doesn't have Psi. Untraceable."

The Moderator's face was rigid. He wasn't happy to be challenged...to be called names by an unknown enemy. "What does this have to do with The Surfer?" he asked.

IRIS—THE WORLD HAS BEEN SHITTY UNDER YOUR RULE FOR TOO LONG. YOU BUILT A SHIELD OVER CHICAGO AND PUT A BAR-CODE IN OUR HEADS. YOU CHEATED. YOU GET THAT, DON'T YOU, YOU IDIOT? YOU TOOK THE WORLD BECAUSE YOU CHEATED. THE LEAST

YOU CAN DO IS GIVE US A CHANCE TO TAKE IT BACK.

"Tell you what Iris. You come to me and I'll give you Rainbow personally. If you can get it to Vegas and plug it in yourself, then you win."

IRIS—I'M NOT DUMB.

"Then what do you propose?"

IRIS—GIVE IT TO SOMEONE ELSE.

"Who?"

IRIS—ARE YOU ACCEPTING MY CHALLENGE???

"Maybe."

IRIS—I WANT AN AGREEMENT.

The Moderator's neck twitched and he clenched his teeth while he gained his composure. "First, you don't get to make demands. Second, if you're making a suggestion, you shouldn't be so vague. I'm willing to take you up on your challenge, but tell me what it is you want."

The dash flashed for a few moments. Everyone watched silently. The Surfer had risen to his feet, watching in fascination and hope. Finally, a ding.

IRIS—I'LL GIVE YOU A NAME AND YOU GIVE HIM THE RAINBOW. IF HE SUCCESSFULLY TAKES IT TO THE MAINFRAME THAT CAN DESTROY PSI, WE WIN.

"What's to stop me from sending people after them?"

IRIS—NOTHING. I ASSUME YOU WILL. BUT I CHALLENGE YOU TO PLAY FAIR.

"We'll iron out the details later. I assume if we catch this person, you'll accept defeat without crying about it?"

IRIS—IF YOU CATCH THIS PERSON, YOU CAN PUT A BULLET IN THEIR AND THE SURFER'S HEADS. I DON'T HAVE ANYTHING INVESTED IN THIS BECAUSE PSI HAS ALREADY RUINED MY LIFE AND I WILL NEVER RECOVER. I ONLY CHALLENGE YOU, BECAUSE YOU USED TO BE A PERSON, RIGHT? IF YOU'RE DEMANDING PEOPLE TO TREAT YOU LIKE A GOD, THEN PLAY FAIR…

"Give me a name and I'll send them out with The Rainbow. The Surfer and Wigeon are off the table though. Pick your candidate and I will give them a fair shot, but understand that when they are caught, I will have Rainbow destroyed."

The Surfer watched the screen, hypnotized by it. He didn't know if he even knew who Iris was, but she was smart. She knew what she was doing. He just hoped she had someone in mind who really could get an impossible job done. He hoped she'd pick The Guide, or The Wrestler, who was one of his more athletic warriors, or anyone on team Surfer.

IRIS—THE TROLL...

"The Troll?" The Moderator asked, his brow creasing. "Did I hear that right? Troll?"

IRIS—THE TROLL WILL GET THE JOB DONE.

CHAPTER 4

The Troll spoke with his fingers. He spent more time typing than talking, and even when he talked, his hands would motion the act of typing. In fact, he was incapable of talking without moving his fingers because before the words were out of his mouth, he was thinking about typing them and felt the impulse to reenact the sensation.

He was only comfortable with keyboard and mouse in hand. When he woke up in the morning, he rushed to the Boards. Most of the Midwest was filled with warehouses that housed members of the Boards. When the world shut down, access to information was limited, but computers were accessible, only to interact with other people via the Boards, which were closely monitored by the good folks in Chicago.

The Boards were a kind of comfort zone for the bulk of population who needed interaction, but didn't want to live in the world without technology. The Troll was an appropriate name for Bobby Bryson. Long before Psi, he would frequent all the big message boards—the ones with heavy traffic—and he would antagonize the masses, whether it be teenage girls who were head over heals in love with the latest boy band, or fans of the films he hated. Politics, religion, the media, social topics, ethics, paranormal beliefs, people who love poetry; No topic was too big or small for The Troll to make an appearance, take the unpopular opinion, play devil's advocate, and rile the other users.

He was, to the Boards, an asshole, a provoker…a troll.

Then the world ended and everyone began going by labels instead of names, and he happily and proudly took the name before anyone else could grab it up, but no one else wanted to be called The Troll.

Of all the fights he instigated, there was one topic he refused to address, and that was the moral implications of Psi, the revolution of Surfer and Wigeon, and Circular Prime. He had Psi injected at a young age, younger than most, and loved it. Suddenly, he was sitting in his basement, watching Westerns and interacting on message boards just by navigating with his mind. Throughout it all, his fingers typed away at thin air.

The takeover by the disgruntled engineers at Circular Prime was a sensitive subject. There had been too many stories of people who conveniently disappeared or had a stroke in the night for speaking out against Psi. The revolutionaries in the early days after the shutdown were dead before they could start a revolution. The idea of an uprising often prompted The Moderator to deactivate the minds of the rebels. It seemed that the only way to survive was to agree, and the Troll had too much work to do. He wasn't much use to his world dead.

He wore a black hoody all the time and didn't groom himself, which was too bad, because if he did, he might have been considered cute, maybe even attractive, but he abandoned those types of desires years ago. People generally didn't like him because he liked to speak his opinion in a loud voice and condescend those he spoke to. For a 26 year old who stood at 5'6, he had a way of making people around him feel small.

The Troll spoke fast. He moved faster. He was a man who appeared to always have an agenda, more to do, more to say, not enough time to say it. His hair was a mess and rarely cut. There was a puffiness under his eyes which had formed from too many days staring at a screen and those days would have never ended if not for Iris's nod in his direction.

The day after The Surfer's trial, he plopped into his chair and readied his fingers with a wide stretch of his sprawled hands. He placed them on the keys and closed his eyes momentarily at the sensation of the keyboard lightly pressed against his fingertips. He let out a breath.

Trolling had begun.

He searched the boards for topics that needed his Internet brand of vigilantism. He found a site for film and television—something no one had actually watched for years, but that people reflected on and picked apart from what they could remember. Though he often agreed with what the users said, he often conjured a good fight anyway. He hammered his point home, made fun of those who had bad grammar, and treated people like they were beneath him. When they snapped, he laughed to himself and would write something to the effect of: DUDE, RELAX...IT'S JUST A MESSAGE BOARD. YOU DON'T EVEN KNOW ME, to minimize their emotional outburst into something petty.

He hadn't watched the trial. He was aware of the fact that The Surfer and Wigeon were caught. He hoped Wigeon wouldn't be killed because he thought she was hot. He declared how tragic it would be to kill someone so hot all over the boards. People screamed in all caps at his insensitivity. He apologized and said he'd take a moment of silence and bow only one of his heads because the other was too hard when he thought about Wigeon. He made everyone believe he was a sexist bigot, a middle aged entitled, spoiled, immoral, asshole who saw user-names as less than people.

He chuckled to himself as he typed, only taking breaks to pop his knuckles or grab a soda from the machine.

Up until the moment a woman named The Chameleon entered his life, life for The Troll was great. He didn't notice as she sat next to him. She didn't type. She just blended in, somewhat literally. Somehow, when he finally noticed her, he could see why he didn't initially catch her in the corner of his eye. She was almost invisible, the colors of everything around her bouncing off the surface of her clothes and skin.

"What the...?" he asked, and trailed off. From what he could tell, she was pretty hot too, except it was hard to tell because her presence played tricks on the eyes.

"You are The Troll?" she asked.

Not many people approached him or talked to him—especially people of this caliber. She had something special—an ability. It was almost as if...

"I'm from Circular Prime," she said.

"Okay?" he responded and turned back to the screen. He suddenly hated that she was there. He knew he'd inevitably one day say the wrong thing on-line or poke a bear and make the wrong person angry.

"Did you not watch the trial of The Surfer?"

"No."

"You've been invited to Chicago."

"Sorry," he said quickly, turning his body toward her to offer his sincere apologies. "I didn't mean it."

"Didn't mean what?" she asked, noticing his fingers moving as he spoke.

"I never mean anything I say on here."

"I don't know what that has to do with anything," she said. "You're not in trouble for anything you did on the boards, though I'm sure it will be reviewed extensively. You're in trouble because your girlfriend Iris threw you under the bus."

"Iris?"

"Come with me," she said. "If you have any goodbyes, say them quickly."

He didn't have anyone to see off, but he considered pretending like he did so he could run. But if he ran from an employee of Circular Prime, he'd likely be tracked and zapped within the hour.

"Can you tell me what this is about?" he asked.

"I'm limited in what I can tell you," she said. He thought she was smiling, but it was hard to tell. Her skin grew more transparent, but when she grabbed his arm, he knew she was no hologram. "The Moderator will want to tell you the rules himself."

"Rules of what?" he asked, trying to pull away from The Chameleon. "I think you have the wrong person."

"You were elected," she said. "You're the one chosen to destroy Psi."

CHAPTER 5

The Troll wasn't dragged to Chicago. He was escorted quietly. The Chameleon got him to a private plane, and just disappeared. It was the first time he'd ever been in a plane. They were only used for important people, but whatever he was being called for must have been important business. They fed him well and treated him like an important guest.

The whole way, he internally questioned what he must have said or done to deserve this treatment. He didn't watch the trial and he barely knew Iris from the boards, but other than that, being in a plane felt like a dream. Not knowing why was a nightmare.

The other men in the plane were friendly enough, but the Troll got a bad vibe from every one of them—as if they thought they were better—and he supposed they were better. They were the leaders of the world who'd tricked them all. The Troll had always accepted that fact so easily, but being face to face made him feel…bitter.

A large burly man with a black polo hugging his large chest appeared. The man's gut stuck out, but was otherwise a bulky man with a crop of messy blond hair and a neatly trimmed beard. He managed a smile, but the Troll saw it was forced.

"I'm The Coach," the man said.

The Troll smiled and made a point to be as respectful as possible. "I remember you. You led The Scorpions to the Super-Bowl in 55."

The Coach smiled genuinely as he recalled the memory. "That was a good year."

"So what is this?" The Troll asked. "Did I do something wrong?"

"You're not very patient."

"Well…you know how it is. Usually you guys just stay in Chicago and we do our thing, and all I ever do is post on-line but a lot of people get pissed at what I say, so I just want to make sure I didn't offend anyone in Chicago. If I did, I'm really sorry."

"We don't browse the boards Troll."

The Troll knew it was a lie, and that worried him more. Especially because he knew he wasn't being dragged to Chicago for doing something right. He could see it in Coach's eyes. He didn't like the Troll. Maybe for no other reason than he was a board browser.

"Did I do something wrong?"

"You'll have to talk to The Moderator."

"I'm really talking to him?"

"Of course you are."

"Does this have anything to do with Surfer and Wigeon?"

"Why would it?"

"They were caught," Troll said with a smile. "Congratulations by the way."

He sounded like he was sucking up, which was far below who he was, but when he saw The Coach didn't care for kudos, he shrank. He was used to being in control of his world, picking at people until they snapped, or blocked him, or tried and failed to rally against him.

"I take it you didn't watch the trial," Coach said.

"No, what happened?"

"If you watched it, you'd know why you're coming to Chicago. I half expected to have to chase you, but you don't watch TV." The Coach laughed to himself. "You get ten minutes of television a month if you're lucky and you don't watch it."

"I don't need to. I'm perfectly happy without."

"You congratulate us for catching Surfer and Wigeon, but you didn't watch the trial."

Troll froze in place momentarily, trying to detect just what he was being accused of. "I assumed they would be guilty."

"They are."

Troll faced forward, unable to carry the conversation further. They rode in silence. The Coach was seemingly unaffected by the confrontation—as if he knew something more—as if he knew The Troll's days were numbered and anything he had to say was irrelevant. The Troll directed his attention into the cockpit at The Pilot—which was also his name—who wore a white shirt and metal wings on his pocket and stared forward through his sunglasses, focused only on moving ahead. The Troll watched for a long time, waiting for The Pilot to do something: Cough…scratch himself… even glance in another direction. Instead, The Pilot held a focus The Troll would have believed impossible. He only stared into the sky, as if hypnotized by it.

When the plane landed, The Troll was taken to a cab where only he and The Pilot spent the ride in silence. The Troll wanted to ask him questions, but The Pilot was clearly the silent type. He was in his own head, and The Troll was afraid of what would happen if he tried to interrupt The Pilot's thoughts.

They were taken to Circular Prime, and from ten blocks away, The Troll watched in awe. Whatever the reason he was here, he was lucky enough to see sights others had only heard of. The days of skyscrapers and vehicles were long gone, but somehow The Troll had been significant enough just to see what others eyes weren't meant to see. It thrilled him and frightened him at the same time. They drove into the parking lot, which had no guard, no security, nothing…

The few who ran the world were a small group and there was clearly trust. The Troll supposed an outsider could be recruited to join them but it would take a lot of patience and time to earn that trust. The way in which The Moderator had taken over, while brutal, The Troll couldn't help but admire. Few people could do so much damage alone, and he certainly understood the motives behind The Moderator's reasoning. Maybe by the time this meeting was over, he would be recruited to live among them in Chicago. He'd have access to electronics, information, technology, steak dinners…

He held onto that hope as he was escorted into the building and to the elevators, admiring every plant and piece of art along the way. The elevator ride was a thrill, and so was exiting on the 35th floor, knowing he was so much higher up than most of the world. The floors were shiny and the walls looked like they had a fresh coat of paint. He could smell it and it was fantastic. The feeling of superiority filled him and he suddenly knew this was where he wanted to stay.

The double doors opened and The Troll looked into a small meeting room. Only two people sat inside and the sight was so surreal to The Troll, that he stood motionless for forty seconds flat.

"Come on in," The Moderator said with a smile and a motion of his hand. Sitting opposite, The Surfer, who was bound, sized The Troll up, a hint of disappointment in his eyes at the look of him. "Have a seat."

The Pilot walked another direction, leaving him in silence. When he was gone, The Troll let go of a tension he hadn't known he was holding. The Pilot scared him—the silence and intimidation, the way it seemed as if he was looking through The Troll...not AT him.

"So you're The Troll," The Moderator said. He looked pleased—almost on the verge of laughter.

"I go by that name."

"Why?"

"It's a term people use on-line."

"I know what it means. It carries a negative implication, does it not?"

"I believe that's relative. It doesn't bother me, so even when people say it..." He trailed off. "It's like when people call people stubborn as if it's bad, but stubborn is actually quite good."

"I agree completely," The Moderator said. He was polite, though he was so wide eyed and twitchy that The Troll wondered how much control he really had over his countenance. "How was your flight?"

"It was fun."

The Troll caught The Moderator staring at his hands. He'd been air-typing on the table as he spoke and The Moderator was seemingly intrigued. He quickly hid his hands under the table.

"Never been on a plane?" The Moderator asked.

"I've never been on a moving vehicle of any kind."

"How was your dinner?"

"Didn't know food could taste so good."

"I'm delighted to hear that," The Moderator said. He seemed genuine, but The Troll caught The Surfer's eyes and detected his annoyance.

"Let's not waste any time," The Moderator said. "I hear you didn't tune into the broadcast."

"No sir. I was busy."

"Trolling?"

"Uh…" The Troll laughed. He suspected The Moderator wouldn't mind. "Something like that."

"Have you heard the name Iris?"

"Uh…yeah. User-name anyway."

"Who is she?"

"I'm not sure. If memory serves me, she hangs out on a few boards. Animal rights…National Parks…all that happy horseshit that some people get all up in arms about."

"You don't?"

"Not really. I don't have a strong position on those things."

"But you interact on those boards?"

"I interact anywhere that people easily get pissed off."

"What do you have a strong position about?"

"Nothing. I just take the opposing side of everything. I guess you could say I strongly favor the underdog."

"Why?"

The Troll thought. "I don't know," he said, meaning it.

"Can we get on with this?" The Surfer finally asked. It was the first he spoke, and he sounded so disappointed that The Troll immediately understood that their revolution—the image they portrayed—it was all a farce. He was comfortable with The Moderator, but The Surfer made him nervous. It confirmed what The Moderator had said all along: It was people like The Surfer and Wigeon who were the bad guys.

"We're having a nice conversation," The Moderator said, defensively before turning back to The Troll. "Troll…something came up during the trial of Surfer. A user-name popped onto our screen. 'Iris'. No numbers or symbols. Just 'Iris'."

"You don't know who she is?"

"She doesn't seem to have Psi."

"Doesn't pretty much everyone?"

"There are few who don't. It was a special moment for this Iris, but in the grand scheme of things, pretty insignificant. She wanted to set a game in motion. She believes that one person could put the world back to the way it was before we changed the rules. Do you believe that?"

The Troll considered for a moment. "I don't know why anyone would want to, but maybe. I guess they would have to be without Psi, but...no...not really. You guys run a pretty tight ship."

"It can be done," The Surfer said with a sigh. "You are going to have to start believing that. Iris thinks you're someone who is worthy."

A feeling of dread overcame The Troll with that comment. Whatever he was there for, it wasn't to be on The Moderator's side. He was being forced to take the opposing position—a position he was fond of in all other circumstances.

"Why would Iris believe you would be right for this?" The Moderator asked.

"I don't even know what this is."

"Have you heard of this?" The Moderator asked, pulling a stick shift from his inner pocket and setting it on the table between them. From the side, The Surfer fixated his eyes on it. The Moderator watched, satisfied in knowing that his foe was two feet away from the holy grail he'd been after so long, and there was nothing he could do about it.

"Yeah, it's a memory stick."

"It's more than that. It's called Rainbow."

"What's on it?"

"The password needed to terminate Psi. If Psi is destroyed, we no longer control it. You've been challenged Troll. You've been nominated by the user Iris to represent those who don't believe in Psi...that want the world to return to the chaos it once was. I granted an opportunity for the opposition, and they were to choose one person to represent them, and you were chosen."

"I don't know why. I don't want the world to go back any more than you do."

The Surfer closed his eyes with deep frustration.

"We've been sifting through your message board interactions, looking for a sign that you are against us, searching for code or something that says you're not just antagonizing people, but it appears that IS what you do. Your interactions with Iris have been scarce, but they were heated—at least on her end. She felt passionately about issues, and your messages were short...funny...to the point...persuasive."

"Yeah, that's all I'm doing. I seriously have nothing against you."

"I believe that, but Iris seemed to think there was something more to you. Or maybe she hates you so much that she wants to get you killed."

"Wait…why would I be killed?"

"Because she nominated you and I promised I would allow this game to happen."

"What's the game?"

"The Rainbow would need to be plugged into the mainframe, which is housed in Las Vegas into a terminal in a room in what was once known as Ceasers Palace. For this resistance to deactivate Psi and undo all the progress we've made, all they would need to do is get Rainbow to that access point and follow the prompts. It's simple, except no one was ever able to get their hands on Rainbow."

"I don't get it. So you're giving this to me and I have to take it to Vegas?"

"Yes, but here's the catch…" Suddenly the Moderator's eyes grew dark and the friendliness was gone. "Ten of my best will be hunting you."

The Troll felt faint. He thought about making a run for it, but stayed planted to his seat. He wanted to protest, to beg and plead, to reason, but The Moderator enjoyed this. He wanted it. It may not have been his idea, but he loved every moment of it.

The Moderator went on. "Here at Circular Prime, my friends and I strive for perfection. We don't watch television or play video games or blow things up for amusement, but we do train to be warriors. We've taken all the values that were once the best values in the world, but in which very few men carried. Values like intelligence, a strong physique, hard work, qualities that weren't prominent in the old world. It was always about money and women and booze and people just stopped caring about evolving. My friends and I have the world wired to our liking and that is why we aren't afraid to rid it of such imperfect immoral people. We keep it in line and give very few privileges. People learn not to always ask for more and the idea of superiority is diminished."

"With the exception of you," The Surfer said, but it fell on deaf ears.

"The game is that I send you out with Rainbow, the only remaining potential to end Psi in existence, and you bring it to Vegas without my top ten bounty hunters capturing and killing you. If they do, they destroy Rainbow and Psi lives on forever."

"No no no, please," The Troll said, begging. "Pick someone else. Get a volunteer or something."

"I agree," Surfer said.

"...Anyone else."

"Let me do it," Surfer said.

"The idea was proposed by Iris," The Moderator said. "I let her choose and you're the guy."

"It's a mistake then," The Troll said. "Like you said, she's probably just trying to kill me for going against her."

"I don't care about intent," The Moderator said. "Someone disrespected The Surfer's trial by challenging me for the world to see. They tried to make a point and I'm allowing it, because, I dunno: I'm a compassionate guy. I even let her choose her candidate. The world saw. They saw a user-name tell me that the majority don't want Psi...that they think I'm nothing more than a criminal. If the world feels this way, and if the world believes that any individual can fight back, then I'll call the bluff and see what happens."

"But how's sending someone on your own side going to prove that? I'm with YOU, man."

"There are no negotiations. I've brought you here. I've fed you. Tomorrow I'm releasing you from the city with Rainbow in hand and I'm taking Psi out of you."

"What?" The Troll said, getting to his feet.

"Surfer and I worked out the rules. If we're hunting you, we're not allowed to track you."

"Please..."

"Stop begging. I've read your posts. You're better than this."

"That's why they call him a troll," The Surfer said bitterly. "He's a big talker on the boards, but a coward in person."

"Tonight we'll feed you well. You'll have dinner with my ten bounty hunters. You can get to know them. Maybe observe and work out an advantage if you're able. You will get a day head start. You're welcome to try to find help along the way, but keep in mind that others have Psi and we can track you through them."

"Why are you telling me this?"

"Because you're at a large disadvantage no matter what you know. This is the best I can do to level the playing field."

"Please…I don't want to die."

"After dinner, you will be spending the night in one of our suites with The Surfer. He'll do his best to coach you. After that, you won't have any contact. Just you and Rainbow."

"And what happens if I make it?"

"I suppose I'll be powerless. We've already taken Wigeon to Vegas and she's there to instruct you if you make it."

The Surfer looked up. This was news to him and it added a new element to the game. Wigeon was waiting, ready to help if all Troll did was make a journey. It sounded easy enough, if only the right person had been chosen. What the hell had Iris been thinking?

"I've read your words about Wigeon." The Moderator pulled up a screen with his mind and The Troll's vulgar words were displayed in message board form, to the disgust of others users. The Moderator read the words aloud. "I'd put more nails in her than a hardware store, Rodger her more than a walkie talkie, give her more Wangs than a Chinese phone book, more cocks than a hen-house, more Johnsons than the witness protection program…"

"Okay, we get it," The Surfer said, disgusted by The Troll.

"He's clearly fond of her," The Moderator said with a smile.

"I was just trolling," The Troll said in defeat.

"You're the guy Troll, and there's no way around that. Trying to persuade me is only going to piss me off and it's going to waste your time. I'm going to get you a nice wardrobe, a hot shower, and a haircut. Dinner will be in two hours. I need you to say you accept."

"But…"

"You're doing it either way, but the world will not be watching you curl into a ball and die. You're going to give them an honest fight. That's what I promised, and you will accept."

The Troll closed his eyes briefly and gathered himself. He needed to go through the motions—at least until he found a way out.

"I accept," he said.

CHAPTER 6

The Troll was taken for a haircut and shave. His hotel was luxurious and the bathroom was stocked with hair products, cologne, and all things that made the man. He cleaned up and admired himself in the mirror, but he found no smile. Instead, his body shook with fear. He felt naked without his hoody and pulled it over his head, finding little comfort. He sat on the bed and waited until he was given instruction. The Surfer wasn't in the hotel yet, which was a relief. He fell asleep waiting, but awoke by a knock and The Chameleon escorted him to what he knew would be the strangest dinner anyone on Earth would ever have.

They walked quietly through the hall and to the hotel lobby where he entered an adjoining restaurant and was taken to a back room. He would sit head of the table—each side with five people lined up who would be hunting him the next day. When he entered the room, it suddenly became too real upon seeing the faces of the bounty hunters. Some he recognized. Others were new. All ten had already arrived, except for an empty seat which was quickly filled by The Chameleon. Her body quickly blended in to the colors around her and she nearly turned invisible. While they waited for dinner to start, The Troll watched as the bounty hunters wrapped up their ordinary discussions. To see the dining room from the outside, one would assume it was just a dinner among an old group of friends.

"Have a seat," a voice said and then the man stood. With The Moderator gone, it was clear who led the group. The Magician grabbed attention every time he spoke, and when he entered the room or stood up, suddenly the rest of the world disappeared, as if by…magic. The Troll didn't know if it was an illusion. Maybe The Magician had fairy dust that was invisible to the naked eye, and being in his presence automatically commanded respect, but when The Magician spoke, everyone listened. "How nice to meet you Troll. I am The Magician, your master of ceremonies for the evening."

The Troll smiled and nodded. He'd already decided his demeanor would be polite, cooperative, friendly…he'd give a human face to the game and hopefully, when their plates were empty, he could bargain for his life. Judging by the looks of the group, he might have a shot. The only person in the room who wasn't very welcoming to Troll was The Pilot, who sat at the far end on the left and didn't say a word all night. The Troll began to wonder if The Pilot couldn't actually speak. He never made eye contact or looked directly at The Pilot. He'd have to win the hearts of nine others instead.

The Magician moved aside to allow waiters to deliver salad to the table. "Tonight's menu will consist of an Arugula salad with caramelized onions, Feta cheese, and Kalamata Olives, followed by one of my favorites: Chinese Duck with Plum Sauce and Chinois pancakes. For dessert, we will be enjoying a cranberry cream cheese tart, The Chef's specialty and award winning dish."

There was some applause at the table. The Troll quickly followed suit, playing the part of a man who belonged in Chicago. He was clearly out of his element and didn't know what to expect one minute to the next, but he'd pick it up as he went along and show the others he was a respectful friend. His foul mouth, sarcastic responses, and poking and prodding were all cast aside. He would keep the trolling in check, as long as he didn't habitually get sharp with his tongue, he would display himself as an impressive asset to team Psi.

"I think the best way to get acquainted would be if we all go around the room and introduce ourselves to The Troll and say a little something interesting or share an anecdote. How does that sound?" The Magician only got a few murmurs, but clapped his hands and jumped up and down wildly with a large toothy grin plastered to his face. He was delighted to proceed. He pointed at the first man in line, another recognizable face.

"I'm The Coach. I know you already know this, but I led The

Scorpions to the Super Bowl. What else you wanna know?"

"Tell him about your team," The Magician said, pointing to a duffel bag at The Coach's side.

"I'd rather he meets the team later," The Coach said. "Assuming we cross paths."

"Okay?" The Troll said, slowly, wondering if that was the right response. He reminded himself to smile, and did, but it came off as phony and The Coach didn't bother to respond. He only sat and turned the floor to the next in line.

"I'm The Acrobat," the man said and shrugged as he tried to think of what to say. "I used to be an acrobat. My whole family was circus." The Acrobat fidgeted and hesitantly sat with nothing more to say. The Troll couldn't imagine being killed by The Acrobat…he seemed harmless…nervous even. Maybe even a potential friend.

The Pilot was next in line, but never moved. He stared forward, the same way he had in the plane. It was scary at first, but The Troll found it annoying now. He wondered if The Pilot would be too focused to come after him, but feared what the man would really be like if he came out of his trance.

"He won't talk," the next in line said, standing and straightening his collar. The man was The Mortician. He had a pale face, slicked hair and wore a black suit. He was tall and skinny and The Troll wondered if he really had wanted to be The Vampire until he found the name was taken. "He is The Pilot," The Mortician said. "I'm The Mortician. Death is a hobby…in the sense that I'm intrigued to know what happens when we pass. I've watched many men die. I look deep into their eyes. I want to know what they see…what they think…in that moment… I am death. My very touch will rot your insides until your last breath is taken..."

The Mortician went on, but seemed only to be talking out loud to himself in a long drawl, pausing between random words mid-sentence. The Troll watched him carefully, trying to find the threat. The man seemed as if he was just a gentle giant…too slow to kill. But he'd watched many die…whatever that meant. He was creepy, but not in a violent way. He finally sat and a minute passed before the next decided to break the awkward silence.

He had a gray beard and bloodshot eyes, and a drunken swagger. He was a mess of a human being, with scars on his face and pockmarks on his nose and cheeks. He was cross eyed and under his cowboy hat, leather jacket, and boots, was a man dying on the inside. "The Gambler," he said with a slur. "Interesting fact: My mama and papa took their lives. Papa first. Used to walk around with a noose tied round his neck. Went to work at the factory with that rope tight around his neck sometimes. Finally went through with it. Mama followed a week later after she shed all her tears. I didn't have the balls..."

He sat down and the room became quiet again. The Troll almost slipped. He wanted to ask "what the hell?" but stopped himself. He'd always assumed Chicago was a little classier, a stronger group of people. Hadn't The Moderator told him they dispelled the bad habits and valued strong character? The Gambler was another non-threat, but The Troll refused to believe that he was supposed to survive this game. Something about this group of people was a very real threat.

The sixth man stood. He was more along the lines of what The Troll had expected. He had a firm tanned body and a neatly combed part in his hair. He stood six foot two and wore a red scarf around his neck. He smiled politely. "I'm The Telepath," he said. "I was one of the founders of Circular Prime and assisted in the creation of the product line. The reason I am called The Telepath is because I have a special version of Psi in my brain. It was experimental, but the design was destroyed when we lost our jobs, but not before I had it injected."

"What does it do?" The Troll asked, fascinated.

"I can connect with anyone within a quarter mile radius. I can tap into their Psi and take over their body by using their Psi to control their neurological system through the brain."

The Troll stared at him in disbelief. The Telepath caught his eye and saw his disbelief, and before the Troll could say anything, his hands were suddenly moving without permission. He stuck a finger into his salad bowl and began to stir it around. He wanted to fight it, to pull away, but his body was taken over. Moments later, he was released. He grabbed his hands and shoved them under the table, afraid to lose control again.

"You see? Complete takeover," The Telepath said. "Psi will be removed from you before this begins, so you won't have to worry about that again."

The Troll understood, but he wasn't worried about The Telepath taking control of his body. It was how he could control others around him. He suddenly had more motivation to stay away from crowds.

The seventh stood, but The Troll barely noticed. He saw movement, but it hardly looked like a human being. "We've already met. I'm The Chameleon. All of my clothes have been engineered using very small mirrors which absorb the light around me. If I'm moving, you'll see the shape of my body breaking apart from my surroundings, but if I hold still, I'm easy to miss and will slowly disappear in the scenery. I was once a calendar girl in magazines, objectified for my body, men cat-called when I walked down the street. I have found that being hidden but strong gives me unbelievable power. There is greater power within than what is on the surface. My persona is proof of that."

The Troll couldn't help but say "wow" and she seemed to be satisfied by his awe. She sat down, but he couldn't take his eyes off of her until the next stood.

"I'm The Poet," the man said. He had wavy hair and a neatly trimmed goatee. The Troll made a mental note to keep his mouth shut and have greater control over his voice. He'd spent a lot of time on the boards talking trash to poets and The Poet demonstrated why. "I am only but a delicate flower in a field of thousands like myself, but I am my own shape and size, my own idiosyncrasies and characteristics that I can see and feel but others can not."

No one was amused, least of all The Troll, but he remained respectful. He suspected if he was on the run and The Poet was on his tail, and they came face to face, The Poet would be the one with his head bashed in.

"I have seen what you have had to say about my passion on the boards that you frequent, and I begged to be a part of this until alas, The Moderator granted my wish."

The Troll blocked him out and his eyes wandered the room, observing the others again. He couldn't take The Poet seriously, but had to play the game for now. When The Poet stopped speaking, The Troll found his eyes again and The Poet couldn't hide his disdain for The Troll. He tried to remember everything he'd ever said about poets and poetry—there was far too much. He wanted to believe The Poet to be a non-threat, but something burned in his eyes…

"I'm The Weatherman," the ninth man said. The Troll watched as a morbidly obese man with curly hair and thick glasses pulled himself out of the chair. "I worked for the government in a previous life on a program called HAARP."

"What's that?" The Troll asked.

"High Frequency Active Auroral Research Program. I helped create the Ionospheric Research Instrument, which is a high power radio frequency transmitter which could temporarily excite a limited area of the ionosphere. What we were trying to do was control weather patterns. We were headed in that direction but funding was cut. The Moderator believed in what we were doing and I'm the only remaining member of HAARP and have access to everything. Most importantly, I have this."

He held up a small remote, with only a few switches on it.

"This little device links to a satellite that can manipulate echos and frequencies with a little control from a combination of Psi and pointing and clicking. I'd love to demonstrate what it can do, but hopefully you'll see for yourself later."

"What can it do?" The Troll asked.

"Create single bolts of lightning, strong winds, rainfall, magnify heat..."

The Troll hadn't been scared of The Weatherman at first sight, but this changed things.

"We were going to use the weather to win wars at one time, create natural disasters that our enemies blamed mother nature for. Then Psi came along and solved all our problems. Now, it's just experimental, but the concept will still work if it's ever needed." The Weatherman sat, smiling at his remote, just as a proud father would. The Troll took a deep breath, the realization that he would be dead soon hitting him all at once.

"The Magician!" the last man said with some fanfare. "Smoke and mirrors, tricks up my sleeve, sleights of hand, more than meets the eye, all those cliches rolled into one. I won't waste time talking about me. Just do me a favor and reach in your pocket."

The Troll frowned and tried to remember a time that The Magician was near enough to put something in his pocket. He couldn't recall, but before he reached, he knew something would be there. He pulled out an Ace of Spades.

"Of course, the trick is better if I make you pick the card first, so let's just back up a second. Name a card."

"What? Just name any card in a deck?"

"Yeah."

"Eight of clubs."

"Reach in your pocket."

Impossible. The Troll had no idea there was so much technology and gimmicky weapons in Chicago, but what The Magician was doing felt like real magic. He reached in his pocket and his index and middle finger grabbed a single card. He pulled it out and the eight of clubs surfaced. "How…?"

"Great magicians are always in control. They never show doubt, never falter, and they never reveal their tricks." The Magician gave him a wicked smile, and though he was just a man without a special suit or a remote control, he felt like the most dangerous of all. "Let's eat," The Magician said.

Dinner was served and it was the best meal The Troll had ever eaten. Four conversations were held at the table at all times and The Troll was never excluded. He talked about his life, shared stories, had some laughs, and by the time dessert was served, it seemed as if everyone was friends—The Poet and The Pilot being the exceptions. The Troll had teetered back and forth with what they really planned for him, but by the end of the night, he realized he'd made friends. No one was going to hurt him. The dinner was being broadcast and everyone could see that Circular Prime and people like The Troll could co-exist after all.

He ate the last forkful of his tart and wiped his mouth. The conversation quieted and The Magician raised his glass. "I'd like to toast The Troll. He may not be loved by the boards, but he's just an average good guy who wants the same things we all want."

They all drank and The Troll smiled wide. "Thank you," he said.

"Iris picked you because you're perceptive," The Poet finally said.

"Excuse me?" The Troll responded.

"I read an interaction between the two of you. It was heated, and you ranted, picking her apart and evaluating her personality based on her posts, and then, even though she didn't agree with you, she called you perceptive."

"I remember."

"Why would being perceptive be reason enough for you to play this game?"

"Do I still have to do that?" The Troll asked, in disbelief.

"Of course you do," The Poet said. Everyone was quiet. "We've all bet on how long you'll last."

"What?"

"The one who kills you will be in The Moderator's good graces and on the side, we've all wagered something on how long you last."

"I thought we were friends."

"We ate dinner together. We're not friends."

"But The Magician's toast..."

The Magician shrugged with a smile. "You can't escape what you were chosen to do Troll. We had some laughs, but we each hope to be the one to end you."

The Troll looked from face to face, The Coach, The Acrobat, The Pilot, The Mortician, The Gambler, The Telepath, The Chameleon, The Poet, The Weatherman, and finally to The Magician. Each one of them was in agreement—each wanted his blood.

"If you're so perceptive..." The Poet said, taunting,"...then how did you read this situation wrong?"

The Troll burned inside. He wasn't used to being teamed up on, outwitted, outmaneuvered in every way. He was backed into a corner, and without thought, he let loose the only weapon he had: His tongue.

"If I'm going to do this no matter what, would you like to hear my perceptions of all of you? Since I'm allegedly usually right?"

The Magician smiled, welcoming it. Everyone else gave The Troll the room, not expecting his board personality to be revealed.

"First of all, I was told that I was here to get to know you so I could have some advantage, but that's not why we're here. We're here so you get to know me. You all want to know if I'm a rebel...if there's more to me than just a troll. That's why you read my messages and pretended to be kind to me and get me to open up. But I really am just a troll, which makes me the most honest person at this table."

He turned his attention to The Coach.

"Your biggest accomplishment in life happened before Psi, so why you're sitting at this table, I have no idea. You're not a coach anymore and never will be again. The men you led to victory are most likely dead because of you, but you still wear your Super-bowl ring, bitter that you can't find a place in this world and are forced to name yourself after a former glory that you'll never relive. Your only bragging right was pre-Psi, so even though you pretend to be with these guys, maybe you're the one we should all be hunting."

He moved on...

"Acrobat...you're so nice and nervous that I don't even want to hurt your feelings. What are you doing here? Are you just a case of nepotism or do you just go along with this because you'll be the one who's hunted if you speak out? This group of Avenger rejects is far below you."

"And Pilot, you had me going at first with the silent treatment, but one thing I learned from the boards is that when people have nothing of substance to say, they block me. You're the dumb one of the bunch who doesn't fit into the big picture and can't keep up with the conversation. You're way of creating the illusion of being scary is to not say anything at all, but in the end, that just makes you a guy that doesn't say anything. You hope people will mistake stupidity for intimidation."

He turned to The Mortician.

"Count Chocula, if you want to know about what it feels like to cross over so badly, why don't you just kill yourself. I would if I saw what you see in the mirror every day."

"And The Gambler, I'm not even going to bother to try to hurt your feelings because you seem to already hate yourself enough, and believe me: You've earned it."

"Telepath, I'll give it to you: You've got a pretty sweet thing going with your nerve control Psi, but I can only think of one reason you'd invent that kind of technology to begin with and don't be fooled: Just because you're tapping into their brains and driving their bodies, doesn't mean it's consensual."

"You wait one second!" The Telepath shouted, but The Magician shot him a look that quieted him.

"Must be nice to be a part of the sausage fest Chameleon. There's no better way to promote yourself as equal and promote girl-power than to cover yourself with mirrors so no one can actually see you. I understand you want to hide how you look, but is there any type of mirrored invention in the works that will hide what's on the inside as well? You'll never be recognized for you brain either

Sugar."

"Don't ever call me Sugar again," she said, her teeth grinding.
The Troll came face to face with The Poet. "I don't even know
where to begin with you. You had to beg to be a part of this thing?
That alone should tell you all you need to know, but you did it
because you're a delicate flower and I made you sad with my
message board commentary? Holy hell Poet, I'm a troll. You reacted
in the exact way you're not supposed to react if you want to defeat
me. I don't hate all poetry. I only hate the 99% of it that's written by
recently dumped teenage girls named Madison or Brittany who wear
black makeup and cut themselves, and how a grown man falls into
that category is beyond me, but I certainly don't think you're a poet
because you know a few words that have been in a few poems. I
think you have the best shot at killing me out there, because if we run
across each other and you start talking, I'll just kill myself. From
now until the end of my life, I can't in good conscious actually call
you The Poet. You will be Brittany."

"You will show me the respect I've earned or…"

"Sorry Brittany, I've got two left. Write it down for later."

He turned to The Weatherman.

"And look at you. You were too fat to take seriously, but you
play at the cool kids table because you get to remote control
everything. That's just pathetic man. If you happen to catch me on
your motorized scooter and strike me down with a bolt of lightening
by pushing a button, is that going to be something you consider an
accomplishment? I know the food around here is pretty top notch,
but miss a meal once in awhile. It looks like The Telepath tosses you
a doughnut every time he fucks your mother just to buy your
silence."

Everyone's eyes went wide and suddenly, just about everyone in
the room wanted to kill The Troll. He didn't react though. Instead, he
turned to The Magician.

"Pick a card," The Troll said.

The Magician laughed, but it was nervous. He didn't like his
own sch-tick being used against him, and was even more unsure of
how The Troll planned to pull it off, but he was enjoying the rant the
most and played along. "Same card. Eight of clubs."

"Reach in your inner pocket," The Troll said, fixating on him.

The Magician displayed a confused smile, momentarily thinking about what could possibly happen. He reached in his pocket and when he pulled his hand out, came up with nothing. "No card jackass," he said with a smile.

The Troll stepped forward and raised his eyebrows. "A great magician is always in control. A great magician never shows doubt. You reached in your pocket. What kind of magician does that make you?"

There was silence all around,until The Poet asked the question that finally silenced The Troll: "Now tell us about The Moderator," he said, leaning in with a smile. It was clearly a trap. To disrespect The Moderator was to commit suicide. The Troll was on a roll and the only reason he was able to go through with it was because no matter what he did, he knew these ten men would try to kill him tomorrow anyway. He'd tried being nice, befriending them, he'd used every verbal weapon in his arsenal until all that was left was to fight back. "Nothing to say about The Moderator?" The Poet asked with a clever grin.

"No," The Troll said. "I have no problem with him."

CHAPTER 7

The Troll returned to his hotel to find The Surfer sitting in the bed, waiting. Something in his face was different—some kind of hope. The Troll supposed while he was sabotaging himself at dinner, The Surfer saw a small victory in his rant. He knew that hope wouldn't last. It was a matter of time before they realized he wasn't going to fight for them, and if he did, he'd be dead within a day. Whatever hope he held onto that they would show mercy was gone. He knew now more than ever that this was going to happen. And his only hope for a plan was sitting in front of him.

"I think you made a strong impression," The Surfer said. "I see what Iris is after here. I don't agree with it, but I see what she's hoping for."

"What's that?"

"The power of persuasion."

"You don't think that could work?"

"Maybe if you were on our side."

"I don't really have a choice anymore," The Troll said.

"You need to embrace it."

"Impossible. I can't accept the situation I'm thrown into. I was perfectly happy before."

"Are you aware that your family and friends were all either enslaved or murdered by The Moderator? You carry in your head the very thing that caused the downfall of civilization, and while I understand why people are afraid to rise up when all The Moderator has to do is fry their brains, I don't understand why you wouldn't fight when they take it out of you and give you the one thing that can end it all."

"If this was a message board debate, maybe, but it's not a fair fight."

"The world will see that. The world sees an underdog without a chance, who also happened to stump ten of The Moderator's most trusted men at dinner. It would have been nice if you would have dragged The Moderator's name in the mud too, but eventually you'll be angry enough. I have a hard time believing that most of the world isn't secretly rooting for you right now. Have you thought about the string of events that would occur if you did happen to get to Vegas?"

"No, because I won't."

"You shut Psi down, making you a hero to 99.9% of the world. You rescue Wigeon, who is every male's dream girl, the people rise up and take back Chicago, recreate the world as it once was— probably better, with you at the center of it all. If you want to retire in the mountains or along the coast, you can do so peacefully. You'll be written about as a hero for the rest of time. How is that not worth a shot? How is trolling on the message boards more appealing than that?"

The Troll spoke slowly, as if he needed to enunciate the obvious point that The Surfer was constantly overlooking. "I. Won't. Get. There."

"If you want to, you will."

"If it were you, how would you do it?"

"Without Psi, you're off the grid. They will count on the action of others with Psi to find you—to see through their eyes. They know you'll try to recruit the populations or find a vehicle or weapon in a museum or a scrapyard. They'll search the grid for areas of movement."

"I certainly can't walk to Vegas. How can that be avoided?"

"There are a lot of resources off the grid that the folks in Circular Prime haven't found. We've found weapons, which we've buried. The world was too big and the guys in Chicago to scarce to confiscate everything. It's all out there to be found. We've squirreled away many items that we planned on reviving when a day like this came."

"And how do I find them?"

"Honestly Troll, if you can get on board, I don't have to coach you at all, other than to tell you where to go first. I have a group of people who will stand with you. There's a man who is called The Guide. If he doesn't find you first, I can tell you where to find him. It's likely that he'll be racing them to find you though. If you live long enough to meet up with him, he'll take the lead. You can hand off Rainbow and go into hiding until he gets it to Vegas if you want."

"You mean I don't even have to do this?"

"Not if you find each other, but I think you'd make a strong statement to the people if you went all the way. You're the face of the revolution right now. You could do it with his help."

"You still don't even know whether or not I'll bother to try."

"I wasn't sure in the beginning, but after tonight, I'm convinced you will."

"Because I did what they asked me to do in there?"

"You went above and beyond. You don't like them. You're not with them. Anyone can see it."

"Yeah, well, I never cared about Psi," The Troll said. "I'm pissed because they're trying to kill me for no reason. I'm pissed at Iris."

The Surfer leaned forward and with a seriousness that made The Troll believe that he just might be capable. "Then don't get killed," he said with a smile.

There was no coaching that night. The Surfer only told him to get some sleep…to stay sharp…to be smart. The Troll looked up at the ceiling and his fingers moved as he motioned typing his thoughts. His best bet was in finding The Guide and letting him take the lead. He supposed if they were to meet, he'd go along for the journey. He was safest in the company of others and on the off chance that they did reach Vegas and shut down Psi, maybe he really would get a parade in his honor and a holiday named after him. It was the optimistic thinking that finally caused him to fall asleep and when he woke up at eleven, he was surprised no one had woken him earlier. He had assumed they were on a schedule, but it seemed as if everything they were doing was by the seat of their pants. It seemed as if they knew The Troll was at such a disadvantage that there was no reason to kick him while he was down. They allowed him a delicious dinner, a fancy hotel, and a good night's rest. It was the peace they'd allow before the storm.

He sat up and turned to find The Pilot sitting across the room reading a magazine, and at the moment The Troll saw him, The Pilot looked up and caught his eye before he stood and waited quietly.

"Do you ever talk?" The Troll asked, rolling out of bed. He noticed The Surfer was gone, which saddened him. No last words of advice and no goodbye. The remainder of his life would be surrounded with people trying to kill him—not assist him. Unless he could find The Guide.

The Pilot's silence answered his question. He waited, but watched as The Troll got ready. "You going to follow me into the shower too?" The Troll asked. No response.

He tried to take his time, wondering if The Pilot would drag him out eventually, but as he showered, he heard the hotel door open and close a few times, followed by chatter from the other room. No one rushed him. They allowed him the time to ready himself, but even the Troll needed to get it over with.

He exited to find The Magician and The Coach had joined The Pilot in his hotel. Upon seeing The Troll, The Magician smiled as if the night before was forgotten. "Good morning Troll!" he said, and out of nowhere, a bloom of flowers appeared in his hand, impressing no one. He handed them to The Troll, who accepted them but tossed them in the trash a moment later.

"We were just discussing a wager on how long you'll last," The Coach said with a crooked smile.

"How long do you give me?"

"Four hours."

"How about him?" The Troll asked, gesturing toward The Pilot.

"Eleven."

"He take off his pants to count that high?"

The Magician let out a burst of laughter. "I don't care what anyone says," he shouted. "I like you. I really do. Another time and place Troll…we could have had fun together."

"Then talk to The Moderator and call this off."

"Round and round you go," The Magician said. "You're talking to a wall."

They led him into the hallway and to a cab outside. He was taken to the city limits where a small crowd had gathered. The only friend among them was The Surfer, who stood with The Moderator, his hands bound behind his back. He watched without comment as The Troll was taken to the gates.

"Give me a moment with him," The Moderator said, stepping forward. Everyone else held back as The Moderator came face to face with The Troll. The Troll shrank, afraid of what might happen. Surely, The Moderator had watched dinner the night before and was displeased. Any amount of good will The Troll had earned by his acts of respect, would be gone, but The Moderator wasn't angry. Instead, he seemed tired and defeated. Something The Troll had done had gotten to him.

"I want to apologize to you," The Moderator said. "I don't blame you for your outburst last night. I asked my men to be respectful, but they seemed to feel the urge to play up their roles in this."

"It's okay...really," The Troll said. What he wanted to tell The Moderator was that his apology was stupid, considering it's far more disrespectful to murder an innocent person than it was to taunt during dinner.

"It's not okay. You know Troll, I'm aware of how unfair this is for you. A lot of people died at my hands once because the world was out of control and someone needed to wipe it out and start again. I used to have nightmares for all the innocent people who died because of what I did, but when I saw the world at peace...orderly and not so materialistic—though they were forced—I realized very quickly that I did the right thing. In fifty...a hundred years, Psi will have just been a turning point that led us to the right place, and while tragic, many sacrifices had to be made to get on that path. Your death is to serve as an example to the rebels out there who challenge us—who try to convince the world that we're doing the wrong thing. Fear creates order, and these rebels clearly do not fear us...do not respect us."

"But why not pick a rebel? Why me?"

"If you ever meet Iris, you should ask, because I'd like to know the same thing. She is responsible for what's happening. There is a way out though Troll. That's why I wanted to talk to you."

The Troll's eyes lit up. "Okay...I'll do it. I don't care what it is."

"Do you know what this is?" The Moderator asked. He held up a small device that looked like what people once used as web-cams.

"It looks like those things they have on all the towers."

"That's right. We need these to transmit and receive signals. This is how we give you music and televise events and messages. Most only receive. The rebels have gotten a hold of a few that transmit in the past, but as far as we know, they no longer have that capability. I'm going to give you one though."

"Why?" The Troll asked, taking the transmitter in his hand delicately.

"There may be people in this world that are hoping you pass this challenge. They believe you're on their side, and though misdirected, they hope you can break Psi. Of course, you and I know that would be a bad thing, right?"

"Yeah, of course."

"There's a way we can accept Iris's challenge, save your life, and diminish the hopes of the rebels who want to fight us to bring the world back into chaos and anarchy. There's a way we can assure that Psi lives on forever."

"Name it and I'll do it."

"Walk a couple hours or so. My men have been instructed not to touch you today. That gives you some time to prepare for this. Get near a tower, transmit, and denounce the revolution. Tell the world you believe in Psi. Destroy the Rainbow live for all to see."

"Really? That's it?"

"If you do that, we will bring you back to Circular Prime and you will be a part of our community. You can spend the rest of your days on the Boards if you wish. We'd only ask that you never speak out against us. We would expect your loyalty. All you have to do is use your power of persuasion to convince the world that the idea was foolish…that you love the world as it is…and destroy the only hope they have in front of their very eyes. You'll be a hero Troll, and you'll eat and sleep like a king for the rest of your life."

"Holy shit…" The Troll said. His world had suddenly turned right-side up and hope was restored. Not just hope, but glory. In less than a minute, he was told that not only would he live…he'd live in Chicago. "Yeah, I'll do it. I'll do it now."

"Wait a couple hours. Let this thing begin at the very least."

"Of course," Troll said, eagerly.

"If you don't do it by midnight, I'll understand there was a setback, but at that point, my men will come after you. If at any point in time you want to call it off, just transmit and do as I've instructed.

Understand?"

The Troll nodded with a smile.

"Perception is everything," The Moderator said. "If you so much as give one of my friends a paper-cut, the world will doubt us. No matter what happens, see to it that Circular Prime doesn't lose the reputation we've built for ourselves."

The Troll was too busy nodding in agreement to fully understand.

Moments later, The Moderator walked him to the starting line. The Mentalist approached without a word and held a machine that looked like a supermarket scanner. He held it to The Troll's head for twenty seconds until it beeped. Then he walked away.

"You no longer have Psi," The Moderator said.

The Troll closed his eyes, feeling empty without Psi. He felt no different physically. He scanned the faces of those who were present —all ten bounty hunters watched; all likely knew they weren't to kill The Troll, but most seemed as if they still wanted to.

"Whenever you're ready Troll," The Moderator said.

Just like that, he was off. He took a step. And then another. Soon, the gate was at a distance. When it was, The Troll allowed himself to breath, and the air felt great.

The Troll only walked for an hour, long enough to put a little distance between himself and the city. He could still see the skyscrapers on the horizon. He sat on the ground and looked toward Chicago. The whole charade was silly. Even without ten people hunting him for sport, he would never reach Vegas on foot. He'd weighed his options just for something to think about. The Moderator and The Surfer each said he would be a hero to their cause if he played along, but The Troll ultimately had to decide, and the decision had been made easy.

There was still a bit of a nagging feeling eating at him. The Surfer didn't seem to think much of The Troll, but all he wanted was the world restored in the name of freedom. Before Psi, every news station in every city, every hour of the day, reported constant stories of murder and mayhem, war and hatred, abuse and revenge. It was sickening, but most people believed they were removed from it—that it couldn't happen to them.

When The Troll's parents were attacked and murdered for the

money in their pockets outside their home one night, The Troll searched for a reason other than a simple mugging, but that was the reality he was forced to live with. The world was filled with bad people and good people were always victimized by them. When Psi took over everyone's brains, it seemed like an attack, but within 2 months, there was order. No one could get away with anything, and since people would still kill only to be zapped and killed by The Moderator within moments, The Troll realized that all the lives lost were in the name of a better world—much like the story in the old Bible where God wiped out the world with a flood. Poison had spread all over and to get rid of it, many lives were lost, but the poison disappeared with it.

The Surfer just saw things differently. The Troll didn't fault him, but he couldn't get in line with his way of thinking. In addition, the only guaranteed way to live a long life was to transmit the signal and destroy Rainbow. Even without the temptation of becoming a citizen of Circular Prime, the only sensible thing to do was transmit. He hated to disappoint The Surfer and his followers, and especially the sexy Wigeon, but anyone in his shoes would do the same.

In the distance, he saw a tower. The remainder of this journey would be easy—a short walk—half a mile at the most, turn on the transmitter, make a statement, and live in paradise. He smiled to himself as he pulled himself to his feet and started the last of his trek, only thinking about what his new life would entail. Good food, prestige, and endless amounts of message board fun. He decided he would take things up a notch. He would be invincible, able to poke and prod away at the posters and tear their opinions into shreds. He'd antagonize them, make them cry, make them type in all caps, and he'd eat roast duck and laugh gleefully.

He ascended a hill and looked up at the tower. All that was left to do was transmit. He pulled the Rainbow from one pocket and turned it in his hands. He held the key to ending Psi and was moments away from destroying it. Never in The Troll's life would he have ever believed himself to do something so significant.

He reached in his inner pocket for the transmitter.

"Hey," a voice said.

The Troll turned, afraid to find one of the bounty hunters there—afraid The Pilot wasn't going to follow the rules and would just kill him instead. Or maybe it was The Poet, ready for revenge. Instead, he came face to face with a man he'd never seen before—a man who clearly wasn't part of Circular Prime.

"I'm The Guide. I assume Surfer told you to find me."

"Yeah…" The Troll said, letting the transmitter fall back into his pocket. At the moment, he wouldn't be able to destroy Rainbow and the thought made him clam up, displeased to be set back. Especially by someone that might not be so easy to get rid of.

"Good job coming this far," The Guide said with a smile. "If you give me Rainbow, I'll take it from here."

CHAPTER 1

When The Troll didn't easily hand over Rainbow, The Guide convinced him to start walking to put as much distance between them and the bounty hunters as possible.

The first thing the men at Circular Prime were going to do was follow the paths, and The Guide didn't want them to be discovered within moments of their departure. "We need to go in the direction that seems as if there is no path," The Guide said, and they went on their way through what were once fields, far away from the streets.

When they were on their way and The Troll was able to think about his dilemma and come up with an approach, he finally said, "I don't want any help doing this."

The Guide was taken aback and they walked side by side in silence for half an hour before he finally responded. "I think you will see is that there is going to be strength in numbers, assuming they don't have Psi."

"I know, but I want to do this alone."

"Why not give me The Rainbow? We can split up and throw them off. If you do happen to get caught, I'll get there."

"That's convenient for you," The Troll said. "I get killed. You don't."

"You're holding the single most valuable item that the resistance could possibly have. The fact that you have it outside of Chicago is a miracle. You know what The Moderator is banking on?" The Guide asked. "He's banking on you failing. I watched the dinner and they don't think you have a shot. On the surface, it would seem that way, but you have help. They wouldn't have sent you out with the memory stick if they believed you'd get to Vegas, so you need to be thinking strategy to defy those odds, because once we shut down Psi, they can't touch you. That's your way out."

The Troll hadn't truly considered the possibility of success until that moment. Having The Guide with him gave him a sort of strength he didn't expect, but if he wasn't there, The Troll would have already transmitted and destroyed Rainbow. Getting the job done would be as easy as ditching The Guide at some point, maybe in his sleep, and transmitting when he was alone. But what if he really got to Vegas?

He dismissed the thought. His mind was made up. He wanted to be part of Circular Prime. He wanted his old life back. He resented that he was picked for the journey.

"I take it you know Iris?" The Troll asked.

"I don't know Iris. If I knew Iris, I would have been picked for this."

"You actually want to do this?"

"Of course I do," The Guide said. "Years of trying to find a way just to get into Chicago have failed us, and this opportunity just fell in your lap. I would kill to be in your shoes."

"But if they kill you, what good is it? Especially since they'll destroy Rainbow?"

"Rainbow isn't the only egg in our basket," The Guide said. "The Moderator used technology against us, and he won, but if history proves anything, it's that there's always a better mousetrap being made. We just have to find the hole in their plan and break through."

"Consider that there is such a thing as the perfect plan—that there exists an absolute—a wall that can't be knocked down."

"Whether that's true or not, right now, all we have to do is focus on getting out of here. If we can get to the Mississippi, I can get us much farther undetected, but we need to plan for unexpected surprises."

"Like what?"

"They don't plan on us making this journey, but maybe they

have a fail-safe. Maybe Rainbow doesn't actually work or maybe all ten will be waiting for us when we get there, or maybe they never really extracted Psi from your head."

The Troll stopped in his tracks and frowned. "All they did was put this scanner up to my head and said it was gone."

"Supposedly, that IS the process, but that doesn't mean they took it out."

The Troll went into panic mode and his body froze in place. He needed to get rid of The Guide now, before the sun went down and the bounty hunters were no longer restricted by a 'no kill' order. "You're right," The Troll said. "Maybe we should split up."

"What are you up to Troll?" The Guide asked. His eyes burned through The Troll. It was a matter of time before The Guide kicked his ass, took his belongings, and left him there. And then what? He'd be killed for certain. All he could do was tell the truth: Or at least some of it.

"I don't want to do this, and I don't plan on. I want them to let someone else try. I want to wait for someone to come for me and bargain with them."

The Guide laughed. "They're not going to do that. Are you stupid?"

"I. Did. Not. Deserve. This."

The Guide grew serious and stepped forward, getting in The Troll's face. "Guess what: Neither did any of the millions of innocent people who were killed by The Moderator. You're one in a hundred million victims of this. Why do you deserve to live more than all those who died?"

"Because I complied by the rules."

"Seriously Troll, if I ever meet Iris, I'll kick her ass as badly as you probably want to, but she chose you and as much as it sucks, complaining is a waste of time, because you have two options: You can fight the odds, hope to break Psi, and we'll figure out life from there without being under the rule of Prime, or you can attempt to get in bed with them and I promise you Troll: You'll be killed."

The Troll fell silent and weighed his options. He hated not knowing what he was supposed to do. He always had the answers, always had a response, always gained the upper-hand. The Guide didn't know that The Troll had an out, and he hated having to disappoint him in the way in which he inevitably would, but at least

The Guide would then understand that he didn't only have two options…that he wasn't as dumb as The Guide was treating him.

The Guide looked in the horizon. The sun was setting and the air was getting cool. As the shadows of the day began to stretch, he started formulating their plans for the night. The Troll waited for him to make a suggestion. Eventually he would have to sleep, and when that time came, The Troll could transmit and escape his clutches.

"We need to find a place to hole up for the night," The Guide finally said, to The Troll's relief.

All over the land were abandoned buildings, most of them stripped of their goods by The Moderator's people or the masses. Most of these places were void of electronics, but even those which still housed appliances, were useless because no electricity ran through. A best case scenario would be to walk into a home that still had canned goods or boxed cereal, but it wasn't likely. They would have to live on the land like everyone else, which meant building a fire and catching an animal. The Troll wasn't sure he had the energy, but they had been walking for hours and he felt starved.

In the distance, The Guide spotted a barn and they redirected their walk. "What's the deal with trolling?" The Guide asked. "What's so fun about it?"

"I don't know. I'm good at it."

"Isn't that like being good at being an asshole?"

"You know, the government used to hire trolls to push their agendas and sway people for or against politicians and policies."

"So what?"

"So it was a necessity."

"Because the government did it?" The Guide asked with a chuckle. "You really have a messed up sense of priorities."

"What else am I going to do? Most people on the boards are just worshiping idols of some sort. How's that much better?"

"People use the boards to connect. You try to come between them. You ruin things instead of building them."

"Says the guy who is trying to restore the chaos that the world once was."

The Guide stopped, and suddenly, he was angry. "First of all, the world wasn't chaos. It was free. We were allowed to make choices, and a lot of people made bad choices, but we were at least free to be who we wanted to be and not worry about someone hacking our brain and killing us. Second, the fact that you're not pissed off about what happened to everyone is staggering. Who cares how many people were murdered before Psi? The Moderator has killed more people than anyone in the history of the world. What does it take to make you angry?"

The Troll shrugged as if he didn't know the answer, but The Guide suddenly saw the truth and let out a small gasp. "You want to be with them, don't you?" The Guide asked. "You would have done the same thing in their shoes."

"Maybe not the same way, but I can't argue with a better world."

"It wasn't just bad people who died when Psi froze us all. It was a randomized group of people who needed to NOT be paralyzed in that moment. No one was targeted. All they cared about was the takeover and of the millions who died, not one was selected because of who they were. All that mattered was that The Moderator wanted power."

"Can we not talk about this?"

"Some troll you are. Aren't you supposed to be the one doing the provoking?"

Some troll he really was, The Troll thought. It really was different face to face. He didn't have time to plan his answer or use trickery against his opponent. In the real world, with real issues, facing a real human being, he was stumped. The Troll couldn't wait to get away from The Guide. He clearly was looked down on by everyone that was part of the resistance: The Surfer, The Guide, they all saw him as the wrong pick, and he felt uncomfortable around them.

When they finally made it to the barn, the smell of straw filled the air. The barn was two tiered and musty, as if nothing had been inside for a long time and was left to marinate in its own odors. The wooden beams were strong, and it would be a good hideout for the night. They could even stay for days if they wanted the bounty hunters to pass…maybe weeks if they hoped to be forgotten entirely. The Troll ran strategies through his head of the many ways they could beat the folks at…

And then he snapped out of it. For a second, the thrill of the game overcame him, but he dismissed it and reminded himself of the real mission: Escape the clutches of The Guide, find the nearest tower, and transmit the signal. He was lucky The Guide hadn't forced him to hand over Rainbow, and even luckier that they had found a place to sleep with plenty of time to call off the hunt. He was cooperative with The Guide and tried to get along the remainder of the evening. The last thing he needed was to be discovered for his real plan. They hunted together and managed to find and capture a rabbit. They found a pond with fish and dinner was fantastic. It wasn't roast duck, but as hungry as The Troll was, it could have been.

At the end of the evening, when their eyes were heavy, they covered their bodies with hay and closed their eyes. The Troll kept himself awake until The Guide was finally out. He rolled over a few times to test The Guide's reaction to movement, but he didn't budge. It was safe to say that despite the setback The Guide caused, it should be easy from here.

The Troll rolled out of the bed of hay and got to his feet. He looked down at The Guide momentarily and nodded his head as if to say goodbye. Moments later, he was out of the barn and walking toward a line of trees in the distance. If The Guide were to exit the barn within the next five minutes, he'd be discovered, but it seemed as if he would have at least a six hour head start, which would be enough distance between them. When The Guide woke up, he wouldn't have any idea which direction he headed, but he'd likely assume he went west, toward Vegas. Instead, The Troll would actually be making his way back to the city to transmit. He thought about what The Guide said about his options and wondered if there really was a possibility they'd kill him, even after he transmitted. It seemed to him that The Moderator seemed sincere—that he would be a man of his word.

He approached the line of trees, but stopped suddenly when he heard the crackle of branches behind him. He realized someone was there. "I need to do this alone," The Troll said, assuming he was talking to The Guide. Instead, a woman's voice spoke.

"You're not going to run away from this," she said. "I chose you for a reason."

The Troll spun on his heal and faced her, his jaw wide open. "Iris?" he asked.

"Go back to the barn," Iris said. "We need to talk."

Chapter 2

When the clock struck midnight, The Moderator cursed quietly to himself and rolled out of bed. He paced in his office as the minutes passed and grew angrier with each passing moment. He was positive The Troll would opt out of the mission, and though he still could, it would have been most effective if it had been done quickly. He hated that there was someone out in the world that could potentially be creating hope for all who hated Psi. He tried to guess how many people that was. A few? A lot? Everyone?

It had been a risk taking Iris up on her challenge, but there were so many fail safes in place that The Troll couldn't possibly succeed. It wasn't that he worried about the shutdown of Psi so much as he worried about how the people would feel about his journey. His bounty hunters were out in the world where if enough of the population was against Psi, his friends would be outnumbered.

The group of men The Moderator sent out were his closest friends and confidants. It pained him to know they were exposed to the world and he stayed in constant contact with each and watched the monitors closely, guaranteeing there was movement from all ten of his friends. They were the foundation of Circular Prime, all men who had lost their jobs before they turned Psi on the people. Something about the confrontation with Iris had gotten to him—as if she was challenging him to make him seem like a coward—or make him lose control. He did what would prove her wrong: Comply. Now, all he could think about was all the ways the game could go wrong.

He hoped it would be over fast, and it should have been. The Troll was somehow distracted, or hurt—something didn't go as planned. He had sized up the behavior of The Troll and determined there was nothing more to him than just a troll, who sincerely feared for his life and wanted to be a part of their group. Yet, he'd never transmitted.

The Moderator needed to get some air. He needed to feel strong and in control again. He spent the next hour in his office, which overlooked the city below. He took the elevator to the first floor, exited the building and wandered the streets, occasionally picking up trash and tossing it into the nearest wastebasket. Their population was so small that Chicago was a long way from looking perfect, but someday it would. He was selective of who he allowed in. Everyone would by law be injected with Psi. Populations would be in control, crime would not be tolerated. Only perfection was allowed. Once they perfected weather control, they would wipe out whole cities to keep the population contained and controlled. No one would know these disasters came from Chicago and the world would forever be shaped by what he decided was best.

As the sun began to rise, his impatience reached a new height and there was only one person he could take out his anger on. He walked back to Circular Prime and through the underground passages until he reached what was once a parking garage, which had now been blocked off without a way in or out, other than the tunnels that led to an elevator to the bottom level.

Chained to a pillar in the middle of the parking structure was The Surfer, who lay sprawled on the ground. As The Moderator approached, The Surfer spent enough energy to tilt his head, but didn't react otherwise.

"Is he dead?" The Surfer asked, expecting it to be the reason for his visit.

"Not yet, but it's still early," The Moderator said, his neck twitching as he talked. "Probably hiding somewhere for the night."

The Surfer turned his head away, relieved that at the very least, Rainbow was still intact. He could only hope The Guide and The Troll were together and that all was going well between them.

"How have you enjoyed your stay in Chicago?" The Moderator asked, taunting him.

"With the exception of my night in your hotel, I've slept on concrete," The Surfer said. "What's the idea? You don't want The Troll to know what savages you are?"

"Oh, he doesn't believe we're savages. He wants to join us. He just might earn his way here."

The Surfer suddenly sat up and stared blankly into his face. "What did you do?" he asked.

"It's not what I did," The Moderator said. "Iris picked this guy. It turns out he's a strong promoter of Psi and very influential on-line. Mr. Troll practically begged me to live among us. I felt sorry for him. I don't see him going the distance Surfer. I think he'll opt out, and when he does, he'll be rewarded."

"That wasn't part of the deal."

"What deal?" The Moderator asked. "We created a game. The Troll can make whatever choice he wants. I removed Psi from his head as agreed. I didn't pick him for the journey. One of your people did, and she chose him on the angle that that the world is anti-Psi. The Troll can prove the notion wrong, or not. He strongly believed in Psi from the moment we first met. You were in the room."

"You presented yourself as the good guy," The Surfer said. "You flashed a nice hotel and gourmet food and The Troll believes that's the life you'll give him."

"Who says it's not?"

"Why can't you let him make a choice without trying to sway him? Why can't you present yourself as you really are? A murderous dictator?"

The Moderator crouched down, his back against a pillar opposite The Surfer. "Because I won't give this world up, no matter what you say or do. I beat eight billion people within moments. Forget being one in a million. I alone, executed a plan that took over the world."

"You killed people. They were people with families and friends and dreams!"

"Is that how you see it?" The Moderator asked. He looked up at the wall and his eyelids fluttered. A screen appeared in the shadows and it loaded a desktop, The Moderator's eyes controlling the browsing. He opened file after file until a long list of serial numbers appeared.

"Each number on this list represents every living being left on Earth," he said. The Surfer's eyes darted to the overall count and saw that not even a billion people remained. "These are your precious people with their family, friends, hopes and dreams. You see personalities. I just see a list of numbers."

The cursor ran over the list and randomly clicked one. A profile opened. It had a name, a Social Security Number, followed by a profile. Toward the bottom of the page, the cursor hovered over a button labeled "execute".

"What are you doing?" The Moderator said. "Close out of this."

"When will you understand that you can't appeal to the inner goodness in me? I don't care if I'm a dictator or that millions... billions...died at my hands. To me, this is just another person who did nothing in life. She probably beat her kids or had a drinking problem or consumed too much too often. Whatever her fatal flaw was, without knowing her, I'm disgusted thinking about who she was. She's a number Surfer. She's just a number."

"What do you want with me?" The Surfer shouted. "Just kill me and get it over with!"

The Moderator turned away from the screen, smiled at him, and suddenly the cursor hit the button. And then the screen disappeared.

The Surfer screamed and buried his head in his chest.

"You see that?" The Moderator said. "Nothing happens. A button is pushed and someone somewhere dies. It didn't change the course of either of our lives, so why exactly should I care? Why should you?"

The Surfer looked up, hatred in his eyes. "We're going to end you," he said.

"Who's we? The Troll? I don't think so," The Moderator said. "I think The Troll will ultimately be given the chance to end you. When this is over, you'll look into his eyes as he pulls your profile and I'll nod my head and he'll know that the key to living in paradise will be to finalize the end of your revolution. The very person picked to prove your point will prove mine. Your troll will destroy Rainbow, and then I'll allow him to take your life. And he'll do it all just because he likes how my chef prepares a leg of lamb. You picked the wrong guy Surfer." He found his smile under the darkness in his eyes. His neck twitched. "Have a nice day."

He walked back to the elevator and stepped inside. The Surfer watched as the doors moved. The last thing he saw in the moments before the doors closed was the smile fade from The Moderator's face, and something that looked like fear in his eyes.

CHAPTER 3

As the sun began to rise, The Guide sat on the ledge of the upper tier of the barn while Iris finished telling him about The Troll's near escape. The Troll cowered, working up an excuse as she spoke, but was relieved to find The Guide was more interested in Iris's presence than his own motivation.

"So you're Iris…" The Guide said. "And you've just been following us?"

"For this exact reason…" she said.

"So if Troll's such a liability, why the hell did you choose him?" The Guide asked.

She looked down, and as she chose her words, The Guide took her in with the same thoughts The Troll had when he first saw her: She was beautiful. Wigeon was all makeup and sex appeal, but Iris was pretty without trying. She had brown eyes, curly hair tied back in a ponytail, except for a strand that hung in front of her face, and olive skin. She looked as if her face had opened doors for her and The Guide's first thought had been that he didn't expect to meet Iris…but he certainly didn't think she'd be so pretty if he did. He wanted to confront her about her choice of The Troll, but couldn't focus. He didn't want to hurt her.

"We've interacted on the boards," Iris said. "I don't believe The Moderator can be beat with weapons and armies. I believe it takes persuasion and brains. One person took over the world with an idea. We need to outsmart him."

"The Troll provokes," The Guide said. "That doesn't make him smart. In my opinion, it makes him an idiot."

"When I was on the boards," Iris started, "I remember being awake until early in the morning with The Troll, fighting back and forth. I was emotional, but he wasn't. Even though I believed I was right in the argument, he somehow still won. I followed him after that, looking for a way to interject and prove him wrong, but he stubbornly picked fights with everyone, and usually made them feel low by the time he moved on. Then one night, he is talking to a man who called himself The Salesman. They were talking about values and Salesman said his most important values were family and preserving country.

The Troll challenged his knowledge of the constitutional amendments and reviewed his browsing history and created a statistic for him and this is what The Troll concluded. Salesman spent 70% of his time at work and 30% of his time obsessively following his sports teams. He barely spoke to his children and hardly knew his wife. Preserving his country manifested from voting once a decade, never in local elections, and knowing two constitutional amendments. The unspoken philosophy of his life was to make a nice paycheck selling items, and to spend that money on his house, car, and sports team fandom."

The Troll nodded, remembering fondly.

"He then went on a rampage, but this time, it didn't have the feel of logical antagonizing. It was a passionate rant, ripping into people who tell themselves they're about faith, but pray when they're in trouble, or say they're about the environment but couldn't tell you the origin of anything they've bought in the last year."

"That's great," The Guide said. "You basically tell everyone they're bad people. Nice going."

"Do me a favor Guide," The Troll said, suddenly on his feet and ready for a fight. His fingers started moving and in the moment, he missed his keyboard. "Before Psi came along, what were your five core philosophies?"

The Guide thought for a second. "Help people who are starving, find happiness daily, service to community, improve the environment, and put an end to animal abuse."

"But on any given day, if you listed your actions in order of time spent doing them, your real list of values would look different. Nobody wants to say they're wasting life because 80% of their time is spent working, shitting, commuting, because we were all exhausted from scraping by to get everything we needed that we didn't have the energy to do what we wanted, like going swimming with octopus or making pizzas in funny shapes, but instead we drink a fifth and cry ourselves to sleep every night. And then you leave your therapists office convincing yourself you're not a completely useless bag of cells doing drone work most of your life. You don't actually believe your list of values. This shit fails for the same reason the self-esteem stuff fails. You can look in the mirror and say "I'm special. I'm awesome," all day, but if you're not actually doing anything special or awesome, you're lying to yourself, and long term, that method of insisting the "real" you is wonderful and capable regardless of your actual actions, is toxic. The reality will keep lurking in the weeds. That's why you can ask someone where they see their life five years down the line and they rattle off a bunch of things they're not currently working toward at all. They just assume the future Them is different from the current Them, just as they assume on the inside they're a different person than what their everyday actions reflect. We're monsters Guide. I mean it. Greedy, cruel, uncaring pieces of shit. We all are, and we know it. That item wrapped in plastic you bought yesterday? The environmental damage its production and existence cause will still be felt a thousand years from now. When you decide to throw it out, it will go the way of all plastic and end up in the ocean, right after chilling on a huge toxic pile of trash that starving people in third world countries sort through, looking for something worth selling. But it will still end up on a huge island of plastic in the ocean, where the sunlight will photo-degrade it into microscopically small bits, which are eaten by fish, poisoning them. Every time you use plastic, that's what you support Guide. And that's just the damage from throwing it out. Don't even get me started on the production.

Those animal products you're eating? Yum, right? Well, did you know that aside from causing enormous amounts of damage to the environment and wasting mind boggling amounts of water, it takes 7 calories of plant matter to produce 1 calorie of meat? People are starving on this planet, not because they don't have enough natural resources and arable land to feed themselves, but because that land is used to grow corn and soy which is fed to farm animals, which become burgers eaten by you. Yes, every bite of meat you take is the direct cause of someone else starving.

What's that you're wearing? Cool shirt. Shame it probably contains quite a lot of toxins and was most likely produced under horrible inhumane conditions by underpaid workers who live in the factory complex where they work and are the modern day equivalent of slaves. It's sad and all, but who cares about that when you're worried about that time you saw someone abuse their dog and you were prepared to lynch them."

The Guide shouted unexpectedly, and it silenced The Troll. "Why can't you do this to them?"

"To who?"

"To The Moderator? The population? Why are you trying to make good people feel low instead of using your brain for an actual cause?"

"I agree," Iris said. "That's the whole point."

"What is?" The Troll asked, directing his attention toward her.

"You sit behind the safety of your computer, fighting battles and always winning. It's in your nature to win. I followed your posts and I saw it in you: You refuse to lose. That's why I picked you. Whether behind a computer or out in the world, people like you refuse to let others defeat them. That's why you insulted everyone at the bounty hunter dinner. You knew they had the best of you and you took it back."

The Guide watched The Troll closely, waiting for a response. Iris really had the right idea, but she might have picked someone incapable—someone who tried to run away—who didn't seem to have what it took to face The Moderator. He was the one man who The Troll couldn't even address at dinner. The Troll shook his head slowly and his hands found his pockets.

"I get it," he said. "And I wish I could do what it is you want, but I believe the world is just fine, and I don't think it will ever go back to how it was before, and I don't know if anyone wants it…"

He was cut off by the sputter of gunfire and before they could try to find the source of the noise, two lines of holes in the barn wall suddenly formed and appeared in a line across the ceiling as the buzzing sound of a helicopter overhead passed.

"Shit!" The Guide yelled. "We gotta go."

He didn't bother to question how they were found. He ran to the door and as he swung it open, he realized they were trapped. Walking toward them from fifty feet away was The Coach, The Mortician, and The Acrobat. Overhead, the chopper circled, which carried The Pilot wearing his usual frozen expression.

The Guide slammed the doors closed and ran to The Troll. "You need to give me Rainbow now."

"No," The Troll said. "You can't just leave me here."

"It's all we can do. If they catch you, Iris and I still have a chance."

"We're all getting out of here together," Iris said.

Another line of bullets ripped chunks of wood from the barn and worked its way toward where Iris stood. The Guide suddenly wrapped an arm around her waist and pulled her aside. The chopper passed overhead, but the threat was at the door now. The shadows of three people under the barn door stretched across the ground.

The sound of the chopper blades began to circle back around as The Guide shoved a large block of wood in front of the doors to block them from opening, but it wouldn't last long.

"Come on out Troll!" The Coach shouted through the doors. "You're done!"

CHAPTER 4

The Guide ran across the barn when he saw The Troll reaching for the latch. "What are you doing?" he asked frantically.

"We don't have a choice," The Troll said.

"Are you insane? Stall!" The Guide said.

They both suddenly looked up as they realized the helicopter was circling the barn.

"We're trapped," The Troll said. "We have a better chance if we talk to them."

"Talk through the door. Iris and I will take the chopper down."

The Troll didn't like that the Guide seemed to have teamed up with Iris, but couldn't deny that they were invested in their cause while The Troll was anxious to stab them in the back. Iris was exactly the kind of girl The Troll liked though, and not in the way that he would catcall her from his keyboard. She looked like the girl next door that every guy in the neighborhood wanted. Part of The Troll had been aware of just how consumed he was with the real world—just how unique and adventurous the position he'd been thrust into was. He'd played games on-line and pretended the avatar was him and it was always thrilling, but somehow he wasn't able to find that same sensation. The fear of death was in the way, but as he watched Iris and The Guide jump into action, he realized that they either didn't believe they were going to die, or didn't care. He couldn't understand how a cause could be more important than living. If he died right now, he'd have no way of knowing if they even won. He'd die assuming they'd lose, and it would be for nothing. But he was forced to adopt their attitude for the time being because there was no other option and deep down, he knew The Guide was right. If the bounty hunters broke through the doors, The Troll was likely dead—especially since The Pilot was out there.

He told himself to get on board. He didn't believe it possible that The Guide could take down the chopper, but what if he could? And what if they got away? And what if they made it to Vegas?

"So how did you cheat?" The Troll shouted through the door. It was all he had...taunting...putting them on the defense.

"Open up!" The Coach shouted. "Or we'll burn it down!"

"You don't want me to open the door!" The Troll shouted back. "Because I'll fight you."

There was a long pause on the other side and then the sound of muffled laughter. They believed he was outnumbered, but they didn't know he had company that was willing to fight. They'd have to beat the chopper first, and since there was no real hurry on their end, The Troll knew he could stall for a while. "Who's all out there?"

"Me, The Acrobat, and The Mortician. The Pilot is overhead! You don't have a chance!"

"What will you do to me when I come out?"

"What do you think?" The Coach shouted with joy in his voice.

"I thought you were all supposed to compete to catch me! Why are you teaming up?"

"Who cares?!"

"Who will get the credit for the kill?"

"You're wasting time!"

"Why wouldn't I dumb-ass?" The Troll asked. He wanted to regret calling them names, but for a moment, he realized this was fun. Maybe more fun than scary.

"Because if you make it hard on us, we'll make your death slow!"

The Troll bit his lip, unsure of how to proceed. He was successfully scared. The last thing he wanted was pain. He turned and saw The Guide and Iris were gathering supplies from the barn. Pieces of scrap and metal tools. They were tossing them to the second level in a pile. He was relieved just to know they had a plan. The last thing he wanted to do was ruin it. He had to keep going.

Iris ran up the ladder to the second story and to the corner of the barn where the roof descended and met the wall. She ran her fingers across the wall, searching for a loose board. When she found it, she tugged, keeping track of where the chopper circled at all times. When it was on the other end of the barn, she'd pull until the boards were loose enough that a whole person could climb onto the roof. She kept pulling at boards until two people could.

Meanwhile, The Guide found everything that wasn't nailed down in the barn: Shovels, hoes, tractor equipment, and most importantly: Ropes, chains, and a barb wire coil. He turned from Iris to The Troll. The longer they held the bounty hunters off, the more hope he had. He watched The Troll for a moment, disgusted that he'd almost opened the door.

When all supplies were gathered, Iris joined him as they bound everything together, wrapping barbed wire and rope around each tool until it was one large haphazard net of metal, wood, and wire. "We'll have one shot at this," The Guide said, and Iris nodded. They both turned to where The Troll stood, yelling through the door, but he was running out of time.

The door shook as it was hit from the outside and the wooden barricade shook with each hit. Eventually they would break through.

"Let's go," he said and Iris and The Guide slipped through the opening.

The Troll stood frozen, watching the door and expecting it to burst open at any moment. Suddenly the thuds stopped and everything was quiet except for the sound of the chopper. The Troll looked up and saw Iris's leg as it slipped from a hole they'd created in the barn. "Great," he said to himself and shook his head. They could easily run off without him and leave him to die.

Or he could transmit now. The Moderator had said that at any point in time, he could do it. He felt the shape of Rainbow in his pocket. He knew he didn't have much time. He reached in his pocket frantically, ready to save himself and end this once and for all, but suddenly felt a gust of air whiz down behind him. He turned just as The Acrobat fell into place. The last thought he had before a side-kick knocked the wind out of him and sent him into the barn wall was that the wiry little guy must have climbed the outer wall and used his acrobatics to work his way into the barn.

The Troll sat up as The Acrobat walked to the door. "Wait!" he shouted, but The Acrobat kept moving, seemingly about to unlatch the door. He quickly stood and rushed the man, trying to wrap his arms around him, but The Acrobat side stepped him easily and sent The Troll face first into the hay. "Come on man," The Troll said. "Do me a favor. You were the nice one."

The Acrobat kept moving, but The Troll pulled himself into a running stance and rushed him again, this time connecting his shoulder with The Acrobat's back. Both men fell forward and crashed into a bench, a tangle of arms and legs. The Acrobat was the better fighter, but wound up by happenstance, pinned under The Troll's body. Acrobat brought his free foot up and to The Troll's surprise, kicked him in the face, knocking The Troll on his back again.

Blood fell in a stream and this time, as The Troll watched The Acrobat get to his feet, he knew he wouldn't get up.

The helicopter flew by again, withholding fire as if waiting to see how the men on the ground fared out. The Guide and Iris crouched at the edge of the roof, praying they wouldn't be seen before their opportunity arrived. The chopper flew in patterns, and eventually it would come straight over the roof.

They positioned themselves, holding opposite ends of their net, both with one knee wedged on the roof and a foot holding them in place. "I'm going to get his attention," Iris said, and started crawling up the roof for visibility.

The Guide tried to stop her, but Iris began her climb quickly, her mind made up. It could work, but The Guide was unusually protective of her. When she reached the top, she waived her hand to get The Pilot's attention. He wasn't sure she was seen until the sound of the helicopter suddenly changed and the propellers shifted in their direction. She waived to The Guide and he began his climb, trying to pace himself to reach the top as the chopper did. As he neared the high point, he felt the wind of the propellers. Iris and The Guide found each others eyes and with a mutual understanding, they both stood on the very top holding the net.

The chopper moved forward with guns aimed. They threw the net high and for a moment, it was suspended in the air, the weight of the net fighting the power of the propellers. Then, a chain caught and

—a little at first—then all at once, the whole thing was sucked into the propellers and as they cascaded down the roof to get away, the propellers began clunking and sparks flew, and then halted all together.

The Guide watched as the chopper began a free-fall and he watched in shock as he saw The Pilot, who's face was frozen without reaction or fear.

The Acrobat reached the door and had his hand on the wooden lever when suddenly the helicopter crashed through the corner of the barn, bringing a shower of wooden splinters and smoke with it. It came straight down, but the propellers were stuck in place.

The Acrobat dived to the side and The Troll hurried backward, but not fast enough. As the barn collapsed inward a wall at a time, The Troll ran across the room and dived behind a pile of haystacks. He looked up long enough to see the world darken as it all caved in.

Iris stood outside the remaining wall with The Guide, hugging the wall with their bodies, uncertain of the fate of The Troll and the bounty hunters on the other side.

"They thought he was the only one inside," The Guide said as a thought began formulating in his head.

"So what?"

"See if he's okay," The Guide said, speaking quickly. "I'll lead them away. There's a town about ten miles to the west. Go there with the Rainbow and meet me at the precinct. Make sure it's just you, and The Troll if he's okay, but make sure you have Rainbow. Meet me there."

They found each others eyes again and The Guide desperately hoped this wouldn't be the last time he saw Iris. There was a time that The Surfer and Wigeon were the faces of the revolution, but suddenly he'd been cast into the spotlight and had run into the most beautiful woman he'd ever seen—a woman who fought for the same cause.

"Find me," he said, and suddenly turned and ran.

Iris ducked down and watched as The Guide sprinted for the tree-line. He was halfway across the field, headed for the opening The Troll had tried to escape through the night before, when the sound of The Coach's voice shouted and he and The Mortician abandoned the barn and began the chase. After a moment, The Guide disappeared in the trees, which brought a smile to her face. Thirty seconds later, The Coach and Mortician disappeared too.

Then, Iris was alone.

The Guide jumped the tangles of weeds and ducked under thickets of branches, easily evading and putting distance between himself and his pursuers. He ran toward the left, knowing people instinctively run to the right. Eventually, he couldn't hear them behind him anywhere. The thicket covered a lot of ground, and the longer they couldn't find him, the better the odds were that they wouldn't. The time for worrying about himself ended, and his thoughts turned to Iris. He hoped she was safe—that The Pilot was dead and that she'd be able to find The Troll in the mess.

The Troll.

In all the excitement, The Guide hadn't found time to be angry, but suddenly his thoughts were back to The Troll, who'd tried to escape in the night, who'd tried to open the door for the bounty hunters, who couldn't hand over the damn memory stick and let them end this.

If he's alive, him and I have some shit to sort through, he thought. He hoped he was dead—that Iris would leave without him. He didn't like the thought of them together. Iris had chosen The Troll because on some level, she admired him. She believed in him. She believed in the man who was willing to give up more than the man who brought down a helicopter.

He took a break and sat, watching the direction he came to confirm no one was behind him. His mind spun as his thoughts of Iris and The Troll came and went, but he reminded himself to stay on course. They had to get the Rainbow to Vegas and kill Psi. Anyone that stood in the way would have to be eliminated: Even The Troll.

CHAPTER 5

The Troll kept still and waited until he could determine who had survived and who hadn't. He heard the bounty hunters run for the forest, but had no idea what the fate of The Guide or Iris was and sensed that if he revealed himself, he'd come face to face with The Pilot or The Acrobat. The chopper had crushed two sides of the barn, but there was no explosion and it fell straight down. He feared The Pilot walked away unscathed.

But what if he didn't? he thought. What if we managed to kill one or more?

On the downside, it could be an unforgivable act. The men of Circular Prime were not just co-workers. They were a community. He could be blamed for their murder.

Transmitting might not even be possible at this point. The Moderator had been clear that perception was everything and no harm was to be done.

"Troll," he heard, but it was a whisper, and the person behind it was moving back and forth in the wreckage, searching for him. His ears perked and he tried to make out the voice. "Troll," it said again, and he knew it was female.

He slowly emerged, catching a glimpse of the wreckage before revealing himself to Iris. Everything had caved in on one side and in the middle of it all was the chopper.

Iris spotted him and ran to him with relief. "I thought you were dead," she said, and he knew from her tone that she was happy he wasn't. Because he had the memory stick? Because she liked him?

He was unsure, but when she hugged him, it felt personal—not mission related. He liked the feel of her body pressed against his and became aware of the fact that in his usual environment, this could never happen. The people on the boards who he spent his time with, despised his existence. Somehow, being a troll was important to Iris —more important than anything anyone could be.

Iris told The Troll everything that happened and he couldn't help but be impressed. He'd almost opened the barn door, in which case he'd possibly be dead, but The Guide and Iris had proved to him that they weren't just underdogs—that maybe together they had a fighting chance.

"We need to go," she finally said. "We have to meet up with The Guide."

Something about meeting The Guide was dreadful to him. He knew The Guide didn't like him and didn't want to continually face him. He liked Iris and wished they could conquer the mission together. With The Guide around, he was just a third wheel—the guy carrying Rainbow.

They walked around the chopper slowly, watching The Pilot closely through the window. It was hard to tell if he was alive or not. If not for the steady movement of his chest as he breathed, he could be mistaken for dead. He still wore his sunglasses and golden wings on his lapel. Under the glasses, his eyes could very well be open, watching them with that intense focus he possessed. But as they passed, he didn't move, which told them he was out. He had a gash under his hairline and a solid wall of blood had covered half his face. The Troll hoped he was out of the game, but The Pilot didn't feel like the kind of guy who could be so easily defeated.

The light of the day hit their shoulders as they exited. The Troll turned back and smiled at the perfectly good barn which they'd destroyed. He was seeing and doing things he'd never believed possible. Iris saw him smile and smiled too. "What?" she said. "You like that?"

"Sure do."

"Me too," she said, "But not for the same reason as you."

"What's your reason?"

"Because The Moderator thought this was going to be easy, and when he sees what happened, he's going to know it's not easy. He'll see you've escaped, his guys are injured, and you brought down a helicopter."

"It wasn't me though."

"He'll think it was. You've presented yourself as on his side, but this will scare the daylights out of him."

"We might have killed his friend," The Troll said, a hint of worry in his voice.

"No," Iris said with a nod of her head. The Troll followed her gaze to where The Acrobat was struggling to walk toward the tree-line. His left leg looked to be crushed, and he used a board from the rubble as a crutch.

"What should we do?" The Troll asked, coming to a halt.

"Piss off The Moderator more," she said, a skip in her step. "Take his friend as a hostage."

The Troll watched, perplexed as Iris walked toward The Acrobat with a fearless stride. He did look harmless in his condition, but he couldn't understand how she was so sure of how to do this—how easy it all was for her.

The Acrobat easily submitted, without much choice, but they kept their eye on him. It seemed as if he knew it was better off to be taken to somewhere he might get medical attention. He also didn't seem too invested in killing them. The Troll wondered if he'd even really wanted to go on this mission at all. He thought about fighting him in the barn and how the only thing The Acrobat wanted to do was let the others in. Maybe he just wasn't a killer.

They took turns holding The Acrobat under the arms and walking with him, and though Iris didn't want to talk to him, The Troll couldn't stop.

"If we help you, do you think The Moderator will call this off?" he asked.

Iris rolled her eyes.

"Of course not," The Acrobat said. "Don't get me wrong. He won't be happy about this, but he's not one to admit defeat. Look how he handled losing his job."

"Yeah, but can't you put in a good word?"

"I don't think you're as good at reading people as you think Troll. When The Moderator sets something in motion, he sets one course, and he won't stray from it."

"You sound like you don't like him much," Iris said.

"He's my friend," was all The Acrobat offered.

"So you like that stubborn kind of thinking? You all were on board when he wanted to kill millions of people?"

"It wasn't quite like that," The Acrobat said. "No one knew what the fallout would be. Even The Moderator was shocked when he saw the collateral damage, but it was too late to turn back. When people started to rebel due to the takeover, he felt he had no choice but to shut them down and he only had one way. I admit he was desensitized by it in time, but at first, no one believed that many people would die. Things settled, the heat died down, and pretty soon the world was pretty damn orderly. When it was better, there was no use in giving up or surrendering. We realized we were in a unique position to have eyes on everything and give zero tolerance to the kind of stuff that used to go on."

"No one has murdered more people than you guys," Iris said with disgust.

"He said he didn't mean to," The Troll said. Iris stopped and turned to face both of them.

"The whole world is so used to defending Psi by force and they've been doing it for so long that they forgot why they defend it in the first place: Fear of death. The world was brainwashed out of fear. Both of you very likely knew people who died: Your parents or siblings, teachers, friends…"

"Who was it for you?" The Troll asked. He could see her passion and knew it was very personal for her. "And why don't you have Psi?"

"That's none of your business," she said, walking again.

The Acrobat fell silent and The Troll sensed his guilt. Maybe he really wasn't proud of the things they had done. He stored that information in the back of his head for later.

They walked another hour before The Troll could no longer take the silence and re-initiated conversation. "So there was this one time…" he said. "There was this male pop-star all the girls liked, and there was a website for him and a message board, and all the fans would post how in love they were and how they wanted to marry him. His name was John Melmann."

"I remember him," Iris said.

"Hated that kid," The Acrobat added.

"Yeah, most guys did," The Troll said. "And so I went on his message board and created the user-name: JMelmann1 and started posting like I was him, feeding the girls all the lines they wanted to hear. I had to create a dozen dualies who knew and believed it was him just to really sell it."

"What are dualies?" The Acrobat asked.

"A term the board used for fake profiles. I was basically one person pretending to be about a dozen. At the center of it all was JMelmann1, who eventually was convincing enough that the girls were throwing themselves at me. I started getting private messages all the time, and you know what I did? I finally messaged each one back personally and told them I decided to get them a ticket to my show. John was in Memphis one weekend and I said if they could get themselves there, there would be a ticket waiting for them which included two front row seats and a backstage pass. I don't know exactly how many of those girls flew out there, but the next Monday, I had dozens of hate-mail messages from girls who actually made the trip, only to be turned away."

"Is that supposed to be funny?" Iris asked.

"Yeah, that's actually pretty mean," The Acrobat said.

"Says the guy who probably assisted in executing every single one of those girls, their mothers, and John Melmann himself," The Troll said, effectively shutting The Acrobat up. "I just wanted to point out the power of illusion—smoke and mirrors. I was actually contacted once by a big organization who was getting bad publicity. They wanted to pay me to troll in favor of them and bombard those against them with insults. They wanted a persuasive defender online."

"Go figure," Iris said.

"Back then, you would go on a site that reported news like CNN and the comments below were always politically driven. The world was divided so strongly that you were one or the other and one side hated the other and there was no gray area. Group A believed everything group B said was 100% wrong and vice versa. You could have everything in common with someone, but if you didn't vote the same, there was an unbreakable dividing line. The mention of liking this candidate or that provoked death threats and evil disdain. School kids were bullied and committing suicide at high rates on-line, video sites were filled with teenagers trying to find their fifteen minutes and every comment below ripping into them until they went insane."

"Isn't that what you did?"

"No. I always take my own position. My belief is that there are no sides, and those who believed there was needed to be mocked into order. I didn't hate John Melmann. I just hated the unthinking obsessive types of sheep who believed he cared about them in any way other than what was in their parents bank account. I wasn't a blue or red state, atheist, theist, agnostic. I don't fall into one category. I just hate the lack of resolve and commonality between sides, just for claiming a label and sticking to it without an open mind. The only statement I ever made, in all my statements, was that taking these views so seriously to the extent they did, was so laughably stupid that I had no choice but to mock them until they realized how small their opinions really were. It was to create waves —not ride them."

"Maybe saying that instead of pissing people off would have been effective," Iris said.

"No, because then I wear the label of crusader—of Internet vigilante. People tune that shit out. No one cares about people who appear that they're trying to change behavior, but manipulate them by mocking their beliefs...worked all the time."

"So you're saying that by being a troll, you were just attempting to better society," Iris said, in disbelief.

"On some level. I won't lie. I loved it for all the wrong reasons, but I did it because everyone's priorities were in the wrong place and no one wanted to be blunt enough to say so."

"Is that why you're glad Psi wiped out so many people?"

"I don't dance on graves," The Troll said. "But I don't feel bad either. Most people had petty problems. Psi was a reminder that other things matter more than the latest celebrity or which politician is the biggest liar."

They overcame a hill and their eyes went wide as they saw a town in the distance. The Acrobat let out a breath of relief, happy to be close to rest. His leg would give out if they let him go, and he needed water badly. "What's next?" he asked.

"We meet with The Guide and go from there," Iris said. "He knows what he's doing."

"I don't understand how you intend on walking all the way

across country," The Acrobat said.

"We've got nothing but time," Iris said.

"Look, I understand your position and agree on some level, but you have to see that this isn't a fight you can win. Things didn't need to be interrupted by this quest, and you are only inspiring unnecessary violence. I don't agree with everything The Moderator has done, but this is such a lost cause that I can only strongly urge that you stop now and give up. If more people die or if you keep moving forward, you're going to piss him off, and he will kill people just because he's annoyed."

The Troll looked to Iris, waiting for a reaction. She took a deep breath and considered momentarily before finally speaking. "You asked me why I'm so invested in this fight," she said. "Why I don't have Psi, why I'm even here..."

The Troll was transfixed as she spoke, finally about to learn her role in the whole thing. Something told him he didn't want to though —that if she kept talking, he might find himself against Psi, and he wasn't prepared yet.

"The morning Psi took everyone's minds, I still had it, but I also came across one of those devices that removes it and I had mine removed."

"Did you know the attack was coming?" The Troll asked.

"Nope. Pure coincidence, but I knew who The Moderator was and I saw how much hatred he had toward the world and how dead set he was on revenge..."

"How did you know..." The Troll started, but was cut off.

"I broke into a Pharmacy, removed Psi from myself with the device, I even kept the device, because I knew I wanted to get it out of as many people as possible, and I didn't know why. That evening, my mother and I were in her car, on our way to the mall, and that's when Psi froze everyone. It was dreadful watching my mother behind the wheel, unable to react or do anything more than stare forward. I could see in her eyes that she was aware. She just couldn't move. I didn't know why at the time. So I grabbed the wheel and swerved and the car ended up rolling down a hill and hitting a post below. The driver's side hit the pole and I watched my mother die, the whole time, she didn't scream or move. She died, unable to even talk to me, though she could have if Psi wasn't inside her. I got out of the car and watched as cars piled up and the world changed while no one was even able to scream for help. Later, when I learned what happened, I knew that no matter what it took, I would end this, because..."

The Acrobat's head was turned away but The Troll was fixated on Iris as she began to cry. "Because what?" he asked, softly.

"Because The Moderator knew we were in the car. He knew our lives were at risk and he didn't do anything to stop it. Taking over was more important to him."

"But..." The Troll started, confused.

She turned to him, pain in her eyes, and choked out the words. "The Moderator is my father."

CHAPTER 6

"Something happened here," The Magician said, kicking at the hay throughout the barn to see what could be uncovered. "No bodies, a broken helicopter...The Troll could not be capable of this."

He turned to the remaining bounty hunters. Chameleon stood at his side, loyal to everything he did and said. The Weatherman sat on a bale of hay, wearing jean shorts with his fat spilling over the sides. The Poet walked through the barn, searching the corners for something to piece together the events that happened. The Mentalist stood outside watching the distance. The Gambler sat on the grass with a bottle of booze in hand and his cowboy hat blocking the sun from the deep grooves in his eyes.

The Magician turned and walked to the chopper. He tugged at the door handle for a moment, but it didn't budge. He then covered it with his hands and suddenly a ball of fire and smoke burst under his palms and the latch just fell off and the door swung open. Without word, The Pilot stepped out and walked past.

"Oh please," The Magician said. "No need to thank me."

The Pilot walked straight outside and looked off in the distance.

"Alright, let's piece this together," The Magician said with some flare. "Four people surround The Troll in the barn. He takes down a helicopter and walks off with three. Makes a lot of sense."

"I doubt he was alone," Chameleon said.

"Or maybe we underestimated him," The Mentalist said.

The Poet shook his head and stepped forward. "No no no. Do not cast thy doubt on the illogical, immoral, immature, incredibly useless countenance of our enemy."

"Please stop," The Magician said, simply. He went back to observing the scene and plotting in his head. "Okay, we need a strategy. Let's hypothetically pretend our Troll is more than just a Troll or has an army with him. We need to cover some ground. I'm splitting you up into teams."

The first team was what The Magician liked to call "dead weight" because they were the dangerous, but annoying, group. He wanted them as far from himself and Chameleon as possible, and simply sent them into the woods, where they projected The Troll would have gone.

The group consisted of The Gambler, The Weatherman, and The Poet. The Gambler didn't look like much on first glance, but he was destructive and sadistic if alone with his target. He just wouldn't be trusted to find The Troll alone, which was why he was traveling with company.

The Weatherman was slow and needed frequent breaks because of his weight. He slowed the group, but if The Troll found himself in the same radius, The Weatherman's remote controlled manipulation of mother nature would be inescapable. The Poet stepped in as leader of the trio. He talked constantly, and led them through the woods, trying to track disturbed areas.

The group didn't get along well, and The Poet was the only one who understood that they were the outcasts, which left him more determined. When The Troll's name was dropped by Iris, he did his research and spent two nights reading as many message board posts as possible, disgusted by how just about everything The Troll hated, personified who The Poet was. He hated approaching The Moderator and asking to be a part of the hunting crew, but he genuinely wanted to see The Troll die. His traveling companions would have to step aside if and when that day came.

They were as mismatched as any trio could be. The Gambler was withdrawn and only grumbled complaints. The Weatherman couldn't focus on anything except for his tired flabby legs and the next meal time, and The Poet aimed to be a smart sophisticated leader. He preferred this crew though because he needed men who would follow and come along for the ride. Of the three, The Poet was highly influential and knew if they were all in one place, it would be he who wrapped his arms around The Troll's neck while the others stood back. The only challenge was in being the first group to find him which is why he tried to be efficient. They tracked their way through the woods, but as the sun began to set, he lost the trail. He considered the possibility that a wild animal had caught him, or maybe Coach, Mortician, and Acrobat, but he wouldn't stop until he knew for certain. He tried to think like The Troll—of course he would head west, but he'd stop from time to time to eat, sleep…

When they exited the woods, he contacted a friend at Circular Prime and asked him to map the area. He was able to determine that there were three nearby towns. Of course, The Troll wouldn't have a map and would need to know the lay of the land, but the best thing he could do was follow the population—anywhere where The Troll would find help.

They walked along the tree line for a while, trying to pick up the trail, but found nothing. "He'll have to pass the river," The Poet finally said.

"I need to eat," The Weatherman said, panting. "Talk to The Moderator and get us some transportation."

The Gambler was seemingly exhausted as well. His bottle was empty and as he sobered up, he wore down.

"We'll go to the nearest town and I'll leave you there and head to the bridge."

"You can't go on without us," The Weatherman said.

"You slow me down," The Poet said.

"Troll needs to rest too. He's going to be in town somewhere, probably asking for help. He's not even out of state yet. We have no reason to hurry."

"We will find him first," The Poet said. "Before any of the others."

"Don't make this personal," The Weatherman said. "It's just a job to restore order. We need to root for each other."

"No," The Poet shot back. "I want to find him before anyone else. Contact Circular Prime and find out if there's any strange crowd movement through Psi."

The Weatherman reluctantly obeyed. He turned to The Gambler in search of a mutual ally, but he was muttering to himself. He wandered off instead and pulled hand-held device from his pocket to do his research.

The Poet was left alone, standing outside the trees and looking into the distance. He thought about the barn, the helicopter, The Pilot, and the three missing bounty hunters. The Troll really was more than he seemed to be, and it excited The Poet. He wanted to meet him face to face more than ever.

A mile from where The Poet stood, The Coach and The Mortician emerged from the forest, both tired from the journey and discouraged they didn't happen across The Troll. They contemplated in the same way The Poet did, looking in all directions, unsure of which way to go.

The Coach led The Mortician, who stopped along the way to observe dead rodents, birds, anything lifeless so he could look in their eyes and wonder what the last thing the creature saw or thought was. The Coach only swore up a storm, frustrated at the course of events at the barn. Though he seemed to aggressively lead the charge, The Mortician was the truly thoughtful one of the two.

Once a doctor, The Mortician built his fascination on the trauma of seeing so many die. He'd witnessed hundreds of people suffer when Psi froze their minds, and initially he was filled with regret and shame for what they had done. He had always been a close friend of The Moderator and they set him up with the best trauma therapist they could find, who changed his way of thinking. The Mortician learned to accept death, and thereby became fascinated by it. He studied corpses with scrutiny, but questioned what it was that really left a body to make the difference between awareness and nothingness. Eventually, the attitude adopted was that he wanted everyone and everything dead so they could all be on one side together. He endorsed murder, but because he believed it was a sympathetic act. He was out to do The Troll a favor: To take his life.

"Who are you?" a small voice asked. The Coach stopped swearing and they both turned to find a gawky teenager on a bicycle.

"Get out of here," The Coach said.

The teenager didn't move. He couldn't take his eyes off The Mortician, who in turn, couldn't take his eyes off of him.

"Are you wearing makeup?" the teenager asked, withholding a laugh.

"We all wear masks," The Mortician said, stretching his vowels as he spoke slowly. "We're all borrowing time until the last of the sand falls and our hour is up."

The coach shook his head and turned away.

"Dude..." the teenager said. "What the hell is wrong with you?"

The Mortician's peaceful and slow demeanor suddenly changed and his eyes went wide and his eyebrows fell as if he was hurt. "You treat life as if it's just a toy. You do not understand how delicate we all our—a pinpoint away from our own demise at any time."

"Yeah, okay!" the teenager said, mocking him.

The Mortician's dark eyes burned through the teenager and as the teenager started to say something else, he noticed The Mortician's eyes and quieted himself.

The teenager was suddenly frozen with fear. He tried to say the words, but they came out in a clutter. "You're...from...you're..."

The teenager started to turn, but The Mortician's long arm shot out and grabbed his shoulder.

The teenager gasped as he lost the ability of his legs and they wobbled under him before he fell to the grass. The Mortician leaned down, keeping his hand on the teenager's shoulder. The teenagers veins turned blue and then the skin around them as the poison spread throughout his body.

The Coach went back to scanning the landscape as if this was a normal occurrence.

The Mortician turned him so he was facing upward and looked into his eyes, which transmitted the only sign of life left in his paralyzed body.

"I know you can understand me," The Mortician said as he intertwined his thumbs as if forming a bird with both his hands and wrapped them around the teenager's neck. "What to you is a joke is the very reason you don't deserve this world. Your only contribution in our paths crossing was to belittle. Such negativity has no place in this world and so I must send you on to where you can live anew. We will meet again one day, and I do hope you have kinder words."

His hands tightened and the slightest whimper escaped the teenager and his eyes filled with tears. The Mortician leaned down and searched the teenager's eyes, amused as the color drained from his face. After a moment, there was nothing. He sat there and waited until The Coach shouted for him to follow.

Together, they walked toward the nearest town.

"He was just sitting on-line when I met him," The Chameleon said. The Magician scratched his head and did a final once-over of the barn.

"Alright, let's call this a lucky break for our Troll for now," he said, his usual flare returning. "Chameleon and I are going to hang back and watch the show. I need something from you," he said, turning to The Mentalist.

The Mentalist was relaxed, leaning against the downed chopper. "I'm not going to chase this guy across country," The Mentalist said. "I've got better uses of my time. Find me a nearby vehicle and I'll just get ahead of him."

"I agree," The Magician said. "You're my safety net. I want you in Vegas. Stay as long as you want, pick up some girls, have some fun. If The Troll gets close to his destination, you'll be there and so will large crowds of people. I'm sure you can make good use of the crowd if that happens. It's doubtful he'll make it that far, so get comfortable until we call you back."

"Of course," The Mentalist said, pleased with the direction. "Sounds fun." He didn't enjoy the chase. He hated to be out of his element—among dirt, weeds, and nature. He wanted to use transportation and sit at a bar, talk to a woman. He had no interest in hunting The Troll—only killing him if he had the chance, and even then, he'd just tap into some locals and use them like puppets to do the deed. Sitting and waiting in Vegas sounded just fine to him.

"Hang tight and we'll get you a ride out of here," The Magician said. The Mentalist nodded his approval. Almost all The Magician's business was done. He walked a wide circle around The Pilot and stopped in front of his face. With the shake of his hand, a pair of keys suddenly appeared. He jangled them in front of The Pilot's face. "There's a hangar five miles south. If we give you another ride, you think you can keep it in the air this time?"

The Pilot snatched the keys from The Magician's hand and walked past, headed in a straight line south. The Magician and The Chameleon watched as he walked farther away and got smaller.

"What do you think?" Chameleon said. "Are you bored with this yet?"

"This is the most fun I've ever had," The Magician said. "The Moderator made a mistake though. I'll tell you that."

"Troll won't get to Vegas," she said with some reassurance in her tone.

"I know he won't. He won't be hard to kill at all. What I'm worried about is how all this will be perceived. The barn...the downed chopper. That's not what we're about. This shouldn't even appear this hard to the world."

"They don't have to see it," Chameleon said.

The Magician turned to her, only to find she'd practically disappeared in front of his eyes. The grass in the field and the sunlight shined off her body, creating a blend of greens and blues on her surface.

"The longer he's alive and it takes for us to broadcast and tell people he's dead, the more people begin to wonder if we have control. The Moderator isn't very happy right now, and when he's not happy, he'll demonstrate what he's capable of. He shouldn't have let our Troll do this."

"Then let's end it," she said, stepping toward him, only her eyes visible, looking deep into his own. He stepped toward her and they met with a kiss. In moments, their hands were wrapped around each other and they were on the ground and their clothes were on the field.

CHAPTER 7

The Guide sat in Falconedge County Jail and sat where the sheriff had once conducted his business. There no longer existed any kind of police force, and the prisoners had died long ago, forgotten in their cells as the world around them adapted to a new way of life. The Guide stared at the skeletons of these men, ghosts of convicts that once sat behind bars.

He'd been waiting for almost a day and was about to give up on Iris and The Troll. He wished he hadn't left her behind. The mission had always been everything to The Guide, but in the short time he knew Iris, he grew fond of her. He hated that she might have been caught by the bounty hunters—that she might be with The Troll.

He'd scavenged the precinct, tinkering with all things pre-psi. It was a building abandoned and forgotten, like so many others. After memorizing every picture on the wall, every cell and long dead prisoner within, he'd finally made up his mind to go back. He needed to backtrack and find Iris and hopefully Rainbow. The optimism that he felt after the trial of Surfer hadn't been very long lasting. The Troll turned out to be a joke. They were attacked too quickly and Rainbow was lost in the shuffle. The whole game had just been more false hope for him. When it was over, his friends would be executed.

He fell into the sheriff's seat and let his hands run over the wood, wiping dust with the movement. He wrote his old name, Joey, with his index finger and stared at it for a long moment.

Suddenly, the sound of voices and shuffling of feet as The Troll and Iris entered with The Acrobat between them, barely able to walk.

At once, hope was restored and instead of asking a dozen questions at once, he was left breathless as Iris smiled at him with relief and wrapped her arms around him.

From behind, The Troll watched, annoyed by the sight. When Iris hugged him, he thought it was special. He reminded himself that she handed out hugs freely. So much for the thought of chemistry between them.

"There's something you should know," Iris said, finding The Guide's eyes. "You're not going to like it."

The Guide listened intently, and before Iris could spill the beans, The Troll did for her. "Moderator's her papa," he said, shaking a vending machine with a few scattered snacks inside. To his frustration, they didn't budge, and he wandered off in search of something he could use to break the glass.

As Iris relayed her story, they locked The Acrobat in a cell. He entered willingly, without any fight. His leg was useless and he was exhausted. It wouldn't be long before the group got themselves killed, so he waited patiently.

She told him the same thing she'd told The Troll on their journey into town: The Moderator was a horrible father. He was abusive, power-hungry, self-centered, and bitter toward society. He was that way before Psi, and the monster inside was only fed when the bigwigs at Circular Prime tried to fire him. The Guide felt sorry for her. He wanted to protect her and restore happiness in her life.

The group spent the night at the precinct, allowing themselves to recover from the long walk. Iris and The Guide shared a cell and The Troll fell asleep on the desk. The Acrobat barely slept. He sat in his cell with his legs sprawled out, staring at the ceiling.

The next morning, The Troll awoke and heard chatter outside. The Guide and Iris stood in the entry, observing the town and brainstorming their next move. If not for Rainbow in The Troll's pocket, he wasn't sure they wouldn't have been gone. *I'm no longer needed*, he thought, but could he blame them? He wasn't exactly as gun-ho or passionate about their ploy, though he wanted to be. He liked them, and just as he'd thought of Wigeon so many times in the past and wished she was just a girl who was part of his world, he found himself wondering what life would be like if The Guide and Iris were able to live with Psi and be content. Of course, they probably felt the same way about him, but The Troll was the pragmatic one. Why fight and die rather than find a way to be happy within the world you resided?

He attempted to wedge himself into the conversation, but they were seemingly private. He pulled Rainbow from his pocket and for a moment, thought about just giving it to them and going into hiding, maybe transmitting and begging to go back to his life. He wanted to be on the boards, posting, antagonizing, interacting safely in a place where he could forget his role—forget The Surfer, The Guide, Iris, The damned Pilot and his damned icy gaze behind those damned sunglasses.

He quickly stuffed Rainbow back in his pocket as The Guide and Iris entered the room and shut the door behind them. The Acrobat shifted in his cell and pushed himself from the ground, awake and alert. Everyone was refreshed, ready to move, but first they needed a plan.

"We were talking," Iris said. "We think we can get to the state line within the next few days, and if we can, The Guide thinks it will be much easier from there because we can use the river's current and fashion a raft. We can make progress without expending so much energy, and probably stay away from the population in the process."

"Or..." The Troll started, but trailed off. He had everyone's attention before he could dismiss the thought. "If we have The Moderator's daughter, why can't she ask him to call this off?"

The tension was thick, and The Troll regretted asking the moment the words left his mouth. He already knew the answer, but couldn't resist the knee-jerk way his mind always searched for a way out.

"Because we don't want this to be called off," The Guide said, enunciating his words.

"You guys are choosing a war over compromise."

"There is no compromise with my father," Iris said. "Haven't you been paying attention to anything?"

"I don't see the harm in trying. I thought he was somewhat reasonable."

The silence was long. The only sound was The Acrobat pulling himself to his feet and approaching the bars, as if he was amused by the spectacle.

"I think this is the point where you hand over Rainbow and let us handle the rest," The Guide said. "I appreciate you coming this far and helping Iris reach me, but between us, we have everything we need."

"I'm not handing over Rainbow," The Troll said, though his mind was spinning. What if he did?

"I don't think you have a choice," The Guide said. "I can't trust you and I'm tired of listening to your resistance. Everyone here agrees that you were the wrong choice for this, including you. All you would need to do is hide until we get the job done. Then you'll be free from this. You're safe now Troll—and you'll be safer when we get to our destination. I'm asking nicely that you let us take it from here."

"I can't," The Troll said, backing away and putting his hand over his pocket to protect the flash drive.

The Guide and Iris looked at each other worriedly, as if deciding how to handle the next step.

"I'm sorry I brought you into this," Iris said. "I just thought you'd be more like your board persona in person. I was clearly wrong."

The Troll felt very small—smaller than he'd probably ever made anyone feel. Even asking to come along seemed useless now. He weighed handing it over and knew his mind was spinning toward that possibility.

"You will never be in the good graces of The Moderator," The Guide said and extended his hand, palm up.

"Sure he will," The Acrobat said unexpectedly with a wide smile. "All he has to do is transmit and destroy the thing. If he does that, he joins us in Chicago."

The Troll closed his eyes in defeat but felt the eyes of his companions burning through him.

"What?" Iris asked, in disbelief. "How?"

"The Moderator gave him a transmitter," The Acrobat said. "He can opt out at any time."

And suddenly, every action The Troll had made, made sense to them. He'd always intended on saving himself. If not for that opportunity, he would have gladly rid himself of Rainbow a long time ago. He wasn't just fearful. He was an outright traitor.

"You have a working transmitter?" The Guide asked.

"Yeah…" The Troll said, but his voice cracked and fell to a

whisper.

"We can use it to recruit," The Guide said, his eyes wide. The Troll was relieved he wasn't angry. He was hopeful...eager to use the transmitter for their cause. Except, The Troll had no intention of allowing that to happen.

"No," The Troll said, backing himself into a corner and guarding his pockets protectively.

"Excuse me?" The Guide said.

"I said no."

"What did they tell you in Prime?" The Guide asked. "They tell you that you're actually one of them? To turn on your mission?"

"I already told you," The Troll said. "I never had a problem with Psi. I still don't."

"You son of a bitch. You have no problem with the innocent lives lost... You know where I was when Psi took over? I was in my cab, watching a man choke to death on chewing gum lodged in his throat. If he had control over his nerves, he simply would have moved it to the left or the right, like people do every day. That was one guy and a stick of gum. Everyone in the world who simply needed to react in that moment was gone within two minutes and the aftershocks were worse. How can you have a conscience and tell me that you want to opt out and save yourself and support that man?"

The Troll shook his head, searching for words. He saw Iris at The Guide's side, a tear falling from her eye.

"I don't want to die," were the only words he could offer.

"And you won't, but you're going to give me Rainbow and the transmitter, or I'm going to take them from you."

"Then you'll have to, because this wasn't your thing to do. It was mine. And you don't make the rules. You feel one way. I feel another. In my world, when you can't win a debate, that's called agreeing to disagree."

"In my world, when you can't win a debate, we handle it with our fists."

"Well, I don't have muscles," The Troll said. "I have fairly brittle bones and I'm not a fighter, so since we both can use words, that's the only logical course of action."

He couldn't help but sound condescending, and he saw The Guide's eyes go dark as he spoke and knew he was making a mistake. He realized he'd been shadow typing, which was never a good thing. It usually meant his fingers were speaking for him and he was translating their words. Usually, when his fingers spoke, they didn't play nice, and The Guide's reaction was good proof of that. His fingers began shadow-typing again and before he could find his filter, The Guide lashed out, spinning and landing a roundhouse to the side of The Troll's face.

He spun and his body slammed against the wall and he lost his balance and hit the ground after. His world spun and everything turned into a blur. He was trying to find his footing and focus when The Guide's hands were on his shirt, pulling him into the air and tossing him across the floor with a roll. He was stopped when his body hit the bars of a cell. He looked up to find The Guide coming at him again, and quickly spun and kicked wildly at him, hoping something would connect and send him away.

The Guide grabbed one of his feet but only had it for a moment before his other foot kicked his hand. The Guide's hand let go, but easily grabbed his other foot and pulled him to the center of the room. The Troll grasped at the bars, but he missed, and found himself in the center of the room, being circled as if by a shark.

"Get up!" The Guide shouted.

The Troll brushed off his pants and pushed himself up to face The Guide.

"You don't have a choice!" The Guide shouted.

The Troll's fingers started to move. Shit, he thought. "Iris didn't choose you. She chose me. Probably because you and The Surfer and Wigeon ran your revolution like it was a lemonade stand. Go back into hiding with the twelve of you left who can't fight Psi."

The Guide lunged and wrapped his hands around his neck and slammed him against the bars again. The Troll winced as the pain shot up his back and then focused on his neck. He tried to speak, to beg for mercy, but he was losing his vision, losing the world around him. Iris watched in horror and The Troll heard her shouting something to the effect of letting him go. Luckily, The Guide understood and did, if only because she was saying it.

The moment The Troll was free from his grip, he twirled to the side and stepped into the cell that was adjoining The Acrobat's cell. He slammed the door closed, which locked itself, and in one swift motion, backed against the wall, far from The Guide's grip. Before

The Guide fully understood the severity of his position, The Troll also held up a ring of keys and shook them as if taunting him.

"So what?" The Guide said. "You locked yourself in. You've got nowhere to go."

"All I have to do is transmit and they'll come for me," The Troll said and pulled the transmitter from his pocket.

"All I have to do is leave," The Guide said and held up Rainbow. The Troll's eyes went wide and he reached for his pocket, but it was empty. The Guide had only one goal in their fight and it was to extract it from his pocket. He'd succeeded and devalued The Troll completely. The Troll lunged through the bars, but The Guide pulled back with a smile. Then, he grabbed a pair of handcuffs from the desk, approached the bars, and locked one side to the door, and the other to the bars. A second pair of handcuffs, he stuffed in his sock in case he'd need it later.

"Now you really have nowhere to go," he said. "Except through The Acrobat. Feel free to kill him if you want," The Guide said to The Acrobat, and started toward the door.

"Wait!" The Troll said. "What are you doing?"

"So we can't transmit," he said with a shrug. "We'll still finish this thing, and you? Someday long after Psi is destroyed and the world is free and the revolution is talked about, you'll look back on your role and you'll know you did what you did. That you had a chance to do something better and you were a coward who locked himself behind bars to avoid having a purpose. So go ahead and transmit, and pray that The Moderator doesn't just walk in here and kill you and let the world watch while he does. Or you can use that door…" He pointed to a single door that separated The Troll's cell from The Acrobat's. "You can try your luck with him, but something tells me he doesn't see you as such a threat when you're on your own. Either way, you're no longer my problem. I took down a helicopter you coward. What have you ever done that's even come close to that?"

With that, The Guide and Iris walked toward the exit. The Guide never looked back, but Iris did, and her eyes spoke volumes to The Troll. She looked hurt, disappointed, pained, to see what had ultimately become of the man she'd chosen—the man she'd believed in.

The Troll stepped forward and found her eyes and his own

pleaded with her to forgive him. "I'm sorry," he said. She quickly turned away and she couldn't look at him any longer. In a moment, she was gone.

The Troll hurried to the cell door and unlocked it. He tried to open it, but the handcuff held securely. He kicked at it, shouldered it, slammed his whole body into it, but it didn't budge. Finally, The Troll stumbled back, breathless, and fell into a sitting position, facing The Acrobat. The Acrobat approached the wall of bars between them and stared through.

"Only way out is through me," he said, taunting The Troll.

"No..." The Troll said, his eyes finding the transmitter sitting on the bench. Neither decision looked good.

Doing nothing and starving to death sounded worse.

He slowly got to his feet and stood on the bench. Pangs of pain shot through his body as he stood on his toes and looked through the window. The Guide and Iris started their journey away from him, with only their skills and Rainbow. He wished again that he had whatever courage they had.

"You transmit now," The Acrobat said, "And I will see to it that The Moderator knows you tried to fight them. They'll be dead soon. The Rainbow will be destroyed. This is your last chance to be with us."

The Troll silently sat again and stared through the bars. He closed his eyes and weighed his options.

PART 3

CHAPTER 1

The feel of Rainbow in the palm of his hand made The Guide feel powerful. They'd walked for two days and were convinced no one could be on their trail. The Moderator believed he could control The Troll and track him easily, and he was right, but he hadn't counted on The Guide to find him and take control of the mission. In hindsight, he realized it couldn't have gone more perfectly. There had even been perks: Like Iris.

They talked every step of the way, getting to know everything about each others lives before Psi. Iris avoided the topic of her father, but The Guide could see it on the tip of her tongue throughout the journey. She wanted to tell him everything. He sensed she felt guilty for having been so close to him once without the ability to stop The Moderator before that fateful day. He wanted to tell her not to blame herself, but he could only wait for the topic to come up.

They walked across the plains of Illinois, once in a while hearing an engine in the distance. They'd duck down somewhere and hide until it was gone. The more time that passed, the easier it was to believe that The Moderator would pull all stops to find them. Or maybe they'd find The Troll and it would be over. Except, The Troll wouldn't have Rainbow on him. The Acrobat would tell The Moderator about them and the hunt would shift in their direction. As far as he knew now, Iris and him were still unknown.

Iris noticed The Guide staring at Rainbow with fascination. "The Surfer would be proud of you," she said.

"I hope so," The Guide said. "I don't think this is how he saw things happening. I was his soldier. I was just a backup plan in the case of combat, but most of us believed in The Surfer to one day get the job done by stratifying."

"You're not so bad for a backup plan," Iris said.

"Well, I kinda wish it had been him though. He's believed in this from the start. He saw what Psi was long before it took everyone over. Me, I just didn't get Psi because I didn't care about technology. I wrote everything in notebooks and saw a phone as a way to contact my parents to say hi. Not as an organizer or browser. I joined The Surfer because I had the distinction of being able to. I was off the grid, so I figured 'why not'?"

"But you believe in what you fight for…" Iris said.

"Damn right I do. Maybe not as much at first, but The Surfer is a great man. Wigeon is too, but The Surfer and I grew close. We only talked strategy half the time. The other half, we got to know each other, played cards and chess. He saw potential in me and tracked down everything he could find to teach me how to fight. I watched training videos, read books like The Art of War. I woke up every morning and did push-ups until my arms wouldn't move. I did the same before bed. He wanted me to have value. He was the face of the revolution and he was building his army, small as it was, and he wanted a soldier to lead them if the day ever came that we stormed Chicago."

"But that day never came…"

"No, because we didn't grow like he'd hoped. For every act of defiance against Prime, they'd execute people to remind them who really had the power. We couldn't recruit from those who had Psi because all The Moderator had to do was shut that person down from the comfort of his office. We hoped for a new generation of non Psi users, but then they began monitoring pregnancies and inserting Psi in all kids when they were six years of age. Psi can read the body—detect pregnancy or illnesses, so we couldn't secretly have babies either. Those of us without Psi are too small in number to repopulate. We realized we'd never have the ability to win with numbers."

"My father didn't need numbers to take over."

"That's right," The Guide said. "So it became about building a better mousetrap, but that's what we've been unable to figure out. How do we beat Psi? That became the question, but it made me somewhat useless. His plan to make me into a leader of an army was pointless when the realization that an army as strategy was out the window. So then, The Surfer treated me as a confidant. He didn't want to lose me, but he didn't need the muscle. Just a better mousetrap. When it came to that, I wasn't helpful. I never beat him in chess...not once. If The Surfer couldn't think up a plan, he knew he didn't need to pick my brain either."

"I would say the journey to Vegas is right up your alley then," Iris said. "This wouldn't be the right task for Surfer. In the end, it really did come down to muscle. You're the guy."

"We'll see," The Guide said. "The odds are still seriously stacked against us." He thought for a moment and finally asked a question that had been weighing on his mind. "Do you regret picking The Troll for this?"

Iris gave it serious consideration. "Any other way and we might not have gotten this far. It's like when you shoot pool and you're aiming for one ball but knock another in."

"So I'm your slop..." The Guide said with a smile.

"I didn't even know you existed a week ago," Iris said. "With Wigeon and Surfer out of action, I didn't know a whole lot of anyone who I thought could do this, so I picked the only person I've ever crossed paths with who impacted my thoughts in any way."

"The Troll isn't going to change any minds."

"No, but it's that stubborn way about people that I miss. My father took the stubborn out of everyone. We're all so scared all the time and so no one is willing to fight. The Troll was a fighter. Maybe only in his own environment, but he still had that quality the world needs."

The Guide didn't like how Iris felt about The Troll, but he understood, and on some level, he agreed. What The Guide really wanted was people who could stand up and face their fears. The Troll only fought under cover of a user-name No one could be touched when they sat behind a keyboard and shouted insults. But then again, The Guide had spent most of his time in hiding the last few years too, waiting for his moment. It made him feel as if they weren't so different. He made a mental note to stand up and say what he believed if he ever came face to face with The Moderator. He wanted to do it to prove he was better than The Troll, to hurt the father who hurt his daughter—a girl The Guide admired.

Suddenly, The Guide wanted to steer the conversation to something else. He wanted to talk about them—the undeniable chemistry between them. He felt his hand brush against hers. It had been happening a lot on their journey. Their arms would swing as they walked and once in a while, they'd touch and both would fall silent for a moment as if registering how it felt.

"So Iris…" he started.

Before he could say more, a shadow crossed their path, belonging to someone who couldn't be more than five feet behind them. He turned to find The Coach barreling toward him, a determined look on his face. He tried to step out of the way, but The Coach's meaty hands were on his shoulders and pulling him backward with his force.

Before Iris could react, The Mortician was approaching her quickly, cornering her where she stood. She got into a fighting stance and as The Mortician reached for her, she easily deflected all his blows. A couple of times, his skin would touch hers and she'd feel burning. She didn't have time to think about what The Mortician was, but made a point not to touch him.

The Mortician took a step back and regrouped, sizing Iris up. "Come with me darling," he said. "I won't hurt you."

"Bullshit," The Guide said. He struggled against the grip of The Coach who had his arm wrapped around his neck. "Let her go. We didn't do anything wrong."

The Coach spoke close to The Guide's ear in a harsh tone. "You think I don't recognize you? You ran from me at the barn."

"We were in the area when all that went down. We tried to help you guys. We were trying to catch that Troll you're hunting." The Guide knew they wouldn't believe him but had to try.

"You helped him back there," The Coach said. "Where is he?"

"I don't know," The Guide said. "I ran off alone."

The Mortician tried to move in on Iris and she deflected him every time, keeping her eye on The Coach and Guide. If only he could slip free, they could run, but their enemy had the advantage. She found The Guide's eyes and he was giving her a panicked look and mouthing for her to run. She shook her head at him, refusing to leave him behind. She noticed The Mortician using a hand-held device and punching in numbers. After a few moments, he looked up at The Coach. "Neither has Psi," he said.

"So is this where you tell me it's one big coincidence?" The Coach asked. The Guide stayed quiet, a look of determination on his face. Everything in his eyes was telling Iris to leave and it enraged him that she stayed, well within distance of The Mortician. "Empty your pockets," The Coach demanded. The Guide tried to fight and resist, but next thing he knew, The Mortician was patting him down. The Mortician looked up with a smile and his hand emerged with Rainbow in hand. "Coincidence?" The Coach asked again, with a laugh.

"Run," The Guide said. "Run or they will kill us both."

"Not if you give up The Troll," The Coach said.

"Why do you even need him at this point?" Iris asked. You got your flash drive. You win."

"Because the world needs to see him fail. They don't care about this," he said, flashing Rainbow around like it was nothing. "Until they see his corpse, they will believe he's rebelling against us and getting away with it."

Suddenly, The Guide brought his head back and cracked The Coach in the center of his face. He slipped out of his grip and made a grab for Rainbow, but The Coach saw it coming and pulled away. The Guide hurried back to where Iris stood and grabbed her arm. They turned to run, but The Coach shouted, bringing them to a halt. "I'll destroy this now if you move!"

His voice echoed in the field and then everything was quiet. The Guide and Iris turned and faced The Coach, who held Rainbow between his thumb and forefinger. "If I do it, your chance is gone forever, and I will see to it that The Moderator punishes many innocent people for what happened here today."

"What do you want with us?" The Guide asked, defeated. Iris found his hand and suddenly their fingers were interlocked.

The Coach stepped forward, a sadistic smile on his bloodied face. "This isn't over until we have The Troll, and you're going to be our bait."

CHAPTER 2

The Troll reached for the soda can at his feet but couldn't find the energy. The Acrobat and Troll's boredom had reached a new low and the activity of the day had been to roll a can from cell to cell, attempting to avoid hitting the bars as it moved back and forth. The Troll couldn't do it anymore and The Acrobat was seemingly bored.

They'd tried every way possible to cure boredom and between it all, they spent most of their time trying to persuade each other to submit. The Acrobat would tell The Troll that he needed to just let them out before they starve to death and swear he wouldn't hurt him. The Troll refused to believe it. He wanted to, but bought his time by waiting him out. The time was drawing near that they really would die if The Troll didn't open the door between them.

They'd argued, talked about life, tried to catch bugs and birds, but at the end of the day, The Troll couldn't trust that if the door were opened, The Acrobat wouldn't kill him or bring him to The Moderator to be killed.

The Troll wondered if The Acrobat genuinely liked him. Their first night together, they'd discovered passing the time with word games was effective. The Acrobat listened as The Troll told him about all his online exploits, the people he'd fooled, the games he'd played.

The Acrobat told him of his time at the circus, how he'd gotten there, what his family was like, the electricity in the air when you're swinging from a bar in front of a crowd of a thousand people, the smell of cotton candy and popcorn in the air, the heat of flames below and the blaring of music upon a safe landing while the crowd went wild.

They laughed, they got to know each other, they argued. And after a few days together, they finally grew bored. They were close to a breaking point. The Troll had to make a move fast or they both would die.

After a long silence and both men staring at the can at The Troll's feet, The Acrobat finally spoke, his voice dry. "If you won't come out, at the very least, let me go. Have some mercy."

"How would I do that?" The Troll asked.

"Just slide me the keys. When I'm free, I'll give them back to you and leave."

"If you're free, you'll just tell them where I am, or kill me yourself."

"I'm not going to kill you Troll."

"You can't just go back," The Troll said. "You're in this too. They'll want to know where you were and what you did."

"I will talk to The Moderator for you. I'll tell them you tried to help us until the end."

"I'm not opening the door and I'm not sliding you the keys."

"Then we both die here."

The words hung in the air and The Troll seriously considered. Stalling forever would inevitably kill them. The only way through the door was to find a way to trust The Acrobat. He'd considered sneaking through while The Acrobat slept, but The Acrobat knew he would and slept light, waking up at every noise. They would either leave together or not at all, and if they left together, The Troll didn't know if he'd leave the building at all.

They spent the next hour in silence and The Troll reflected on the events since The Chameleon entered his life. For the first time since it all began, he began wondering why he of all people really stood out. He'd always assumed there were plenty of Trolls on the boards but he'd never known he was the best of them. Iris had been wrong about him though. She knew that now. What she'd needed all along was someone like The Guide. He hoped they'd live and find a way to be content with whatever happened. Vegas would never happen. It had never been in the cards. Not for him or anyone else, but they were survivors. They had that stubborn way about them—the same stubborn he'd fooled them into thinking he had. If he ever got out of the cell, he wondered if he could ever re-establish his persona. Would the users on the boards know he was the same troll picked to restore life before Psi? If so, his trolling days would be over. They likely already were.

As his eyelids grew heavy, he wondered if this would be the time he wouldn't wake up. It would happen eventually. Maybe in a week. Maybe two. One day, he just wouldn't wake up. It wasn't such a bad way to go. He'd probably never know it when it happened, but he wasn't prepared. What he wanted was a cake, or an apple, or a glass of water...

He began to close his eyes, but was shaken awake by a flicker of light that suddenly turned into a screen that covered the wall. Outside, screens lit up in the sky and all over in the distance. The Moderator was transmitting a signal and apparently the message was something for everyone to see. The sky filled with screens and the countdown to broadcast began.

He turned to The Acrobat with a raised eyebrow and The Acrobat struggled to his feet, equally curious.

The Moderator suddenly appeared on the screen, a pleased smile plastered to his face.

"Hello world," he said with a pleasant smile. His neck twitched and he took a deep breath. "As you know, at the trial of The criminal known as The Surfer, I was challenged by a faceless enemy known as Iris. This Iris made the claim that Psi was unpopular with the masses and that any chosen citizen would prove this by using what we have called Rainbow to where it can destroy Psi forever. The claim came with a strong assumption. The assumption was that people would gather together and the population would collectively bring Rainbow to its destination and destroy Psi. Of course, we at Circular Prime see a better world—a world without crime—restrictions that have created peace and deprived society of material things that at one time became gods to everyone.

I am not a fool though. Understandably, some of these things are missed. Surely, you must remember going to movies and watching television and buying CDs and driving cars and flying in planes. I apologize to those of you who reflect on these memories fondly, but I want to remind you that it was conveniences—shortcuts in life—that led people to consume until consumption became more important than relationships. One thing I have never forbidden has been relationships.

We all lost something when Psi created order. It was necessary to...reboot so to speak. If I could have found a way for Psi to act more immediately, I would have. I lost my wife...my daughter..."

The Troll frowned, studying The Moderator's face as he spoke, trying to find in his eyes a tear, or any kind of sadness.

"I wish things had been different, but we needed order and we needed it fast. Psi allowed me to see the habits of the population that are invisible when you live among each other. You wouldn't believe how many of you were living amongst active serial killers, child molesters, rapists, common criminals... They were everywhere, and no one was safe. I can tell you with one hundred percent certainty that you are all safe now. With Psi, I was granted the ability to see horrendous motives and I have been able to monitor and prevent awful things from happening before they happen. For these criminals, there was no judge or jury, no politics or paperwork. A man kills another man, and I shut him down. It's that simple, and it has deterred violence for quite some time. How long has it been since you've needed to lock your doors?

This ability has come at a great cost, but one day when the population has reached its new high, and it is filled with decent people who love one another and not the newest computer or automobile, you will all fully understand what my motivation has always been."

His smile faded and suddenly The Moderator was serious.

"However...," he continued, "...let's talk about The Troll and the journey he was tasked with. The Troll proved to me that the population was not against Psi. The first thing he did was give Rainbow to someone else to carry out his responsibility like a coward. This candidate has been captured along with the criminal known as Iris. They are being held in Heritage Square in what was once Illinois and will be executed tomorrow at sun up for their crimes and Rainbow will be destroyed as a symbol to you—that the sun will never set without Psi.

That leaves one loose end: The Troll.

He has committed crimes of which he will need to pay for. We would like to have him in Heritage Square tomorrow morning as well. The captures, and my dear friends, credited with the capture of

Iris and a man who goes by the name Guide, are The Coach and The Mortician. The Pilot also had a large hand in the search and seizure. I will allow them the opportunity to punish them by whatever means they choose. The event will not be televised due to the possible nature of the punishment.

I would like The Troll to be alongside these criminals. I'm sure he is watching right now…"

The Troll's face was blank. At the bounty hunter dinner, he declined to speak out against The Moderator, but suddenly he wished he had. It might have been his one chance to expose him in some way—to troll the man who wanted him dead.

"…Troll…you have until tomorrow morning to reveal yourself. It is my understanding that you have stolen a transmitter from Circular Prime. You may use this transmitter to give your location up. If you do not surrender to the world before Iris and Guide are executed, I will use Psi to deactivate ten percent of the population and if that happens, their blood is on your hands.

I apologize to those of you who this will impact, but the only way to maintain the peace we've sacrificed so much for is to be firm and enforce zero tolerance for those who try to take it away. I do hope I will not be forced to take such actions and I ask of you Troll: Reveal yourself. When you surrendered Rainbow to another, you failed the challenge. You have until sun up."

The broadcast ended and The Troll stared at where the screen had been for a long moment, his mouth wide open. He turned to The Acrobat, who was seemingly distraught by it. Their eyes met.

"Looks like you have some choices to make," The Acrobat said. "You'd be wise to transmit at this point."

"Yeah…" The Troll said, but remained in his own head, trying to digest everything he'd heard. "We have to go," he finally said.

"What's that mean?"

"If I transmit, they will kill Iris and The Guide and all those other people."

"Not if you turn yourself in."

"But then what?" The Troll asked. "They'd still kill Iris and The Guide. They'd probably kill me. I…" he trailed off, uncertain of what to do.

"Do you think you have another option?"

"I want Rainbow back. I want to try again."

"Not an option."

"I failed because I gave up Rainbow. What if we get it back?"

"What do you mean we? There's no 'we' Troll."

"Yeah, there is. Because you don't like when The Moderator punishes people like this. You don't want him to kill one in ten of what's left."

"What is this to you? How is it that you've never cared about this and now suddenly you do?"

"For the same reason that a decent guy like you can live in Chicago," The Troll said, "Among The Moderator and all those other guys. Because you detached yourself from what you all did. You justified it by looking at how the world improved and disowned the fact that you killed billions of people."

"I didn't kill anyone."

"You see? Exactly!" The Troll said. "You disown it because you didn't push the button, but where was your opposing voice when The Moderator did it? I don't speak out against it because I didn't commit the crime. We're all safe as long as we're not the ones with our fingers on the buttons. We can say "I didn't do it" all day long, but we didn't stop it either."

"You have no idea what you're saying Troll."

"When Psi first took over, I was as pissed off as everyone else. I was a troll before Psi and I initially trolled it too. I was one post into ripping into The Moderator's character when my screen went blank and my head suddenly felt a stinging burning sensation. I thought I was going to die and I might have been moments away, but suddenly it stopped. My computer came back on and the words "Too far... Never again..." were displayed on my screen. They were then deleted and never came back. I was warned, and so I never did it again and adapted like everyone else. And yeah, I saw the good that came of it all, but we've all forgotten what it was like at first and how much pain it caused, and the good that came out of it was just an unintended effect and we used that effect to stand up for The Moderator and call it noble because to call it anything else meant we would just be killed by him. And I don't regret that I never spoke out again because I wouldn't have lived another day if I had, but we can't pretend like he's a great man and that he's doing what he does to keep the peace. He's going to kill ten percent of the world and this time, it will be on our heads Acrobat. This time, in this moment, there are two people in the world that can stop this from happening. He will be the one that pushes the button, but if we don't do anything, it's our fault too"

"I agree," The Acrobat said. "All you have to do is transmit."

"And tomorrow when I'm dead, he'll find a new reason to kill a bunch of people. And next week. And a month later. And you will be eating well and you will know you could have stopped it."

"There is no way to stop it."

"Maybe not, but that's not good enough right now."

"What are you proposing Troll?"

"We get to Heritage Square, help Iris and The Guide get away with Rainbow, and I'll turn myself in. Maybe he won't kill all those people and maybe they can get to Vegas. I don't know, but here's the deal Acrobat...I'm opening this door and I'm walking through your cell. I really hope you don't kill me and I really hope you don't take me and turn me in. I can't fight you. I already know that. But I'm begging you to just get me there. Let me try to reason with the Moderator."

They stared at each other for a long time, The Acrobat contemplating his words. Finally, The Acrobat took a step back, allowing The Troll the space he needed to unlock the cell door between them. The Troll never took his eyes off The Acrobat as he stepped forward and slowly turned the key.

The door slowly swung open and The Troll stepped into their cell. The Acrobat stood still, waiting for him to open the last door to freedom.

"Are you going to help me?" The Troll asked.

"If you're willing to prevent The Moderator from killing all those people, I can help you do it. As for your friends and Rainbow and the journey, I can't help you. Anything beyond turning yourself in would be suicide."

The Troll unlocked the cell door and both men walked outside. The Acrobat closed his eyes, taking in the sunlight with relief. The Troll watched him, enjoying a breeze on his face, his mind spinning as he tried to decide just how far he wanted to go.

CHAPTER 3

Heritage Square was a small town bordering the Mississippi River. It was built to have the appearance of the olden days, when there still existed blacksmiths and wagons that delivered the mail. In the center of the town was a large fountain, surrounded by brick walkways and abandoned souvenir and candy shops circling it.

As the sun set, the fountain lit up and Iris took a moment to realize just how beautiful it was. In the distance, from where she was bound to the statue, she could see the large Sugar Creek Covered Bridge which crossed into the next state, teasing her by being so close. The Guide had wanted to make it to the river and here they were, but unable to move another step.

Her hands were bound to the statue in the center of the fountain and her legs were submerged no farther than her knees, but as the night fell, the water grew colder and she began to shiver. "We could die overnight," she said.

Behind her, The Guide took a deep breath, contemplating how he could make her feel better, but she was right. Their position was uncomfortable, and they were exposed to the world. Any number of things could go wrong. "It might be best if we do," The Guide said. "They don't have anything better planned for us."

"This can't be it," Iris said, grinding her teeth.

"What do we got? The Surfer and Wigeon are out of the fight, The Troll was useless, there's no revolution left, everyone's got Psi...We've never had an advantage Iris. I'm sorry, but that's the reality."

"We still have our interrogation," she said, with some hope. They were awaiting their "trial" which was a watered down version of justice held by The Moderator, who would be coming by to talk to his prisoners.

"I hate to point this out, but maybe The Troll was right about you appealing to your father. He's going to kill millions of people. I doubt The Troll will turn himself in. The only chance we have at stopping this is you to confront him."

Iris laughed. "I don't think so Guide. For one thing, I was a fat little girl the last time he saw me. My hair's different, I'm twenty years older...he won't recognize me."

"So tell him..."

"No. I never intended on revealing myself and I never will."

"Not even with millions of lives at stake?"

"Even if I did, he wouldn't cave. You know how stubborn he is. In his mind, he killed me along with everyone else, and it didn't bother him at all. He's not going to listen to anyone. He's set his terms and that's what he's going to do, because that's how he is."

"Then what's your suggestion?" The Guide asked, at a loss.

"I know you don't want to hear this, but it's times like these that I wish we did have Troll here. You saw him at the bounty hunter dinner, and he did that while he was still in love with Psi."

"All he does is insult people."

"No Guide, you still don't get it. He exposes people, and that's what we need. The public will never know that you brought down a helicopter because Circular Prime doesn't want to be seen as anything but perfect. Once you expose imperfections, you cast doubt. I watched The Troll in so many exchanges on-line where the issue stopped mattering the moment he discredited the user on the other side of the debate."

"Well, The Troll's not here, and if he was, he wouldn't go up against The Moderator. He had his chance and passed."

"He wasn't angry enough."

"He's very likely dead or on his way there. I doubt he'll ever be angry enough."

"I'm just saying: I admired The Surfer and Wigeon when they managed to hack the airwaves, but I never agreed with the tactical approach. It was all about recruiting, but no one's going to join you when everyone thinks The Moderator is invincible. They'll join you when they realize he can be defeated."

"So how do we troll him? How do we expose him?"

"You force him to slip up. You corner him, baffle him, make him falter or snap or lose his cool. All you have to do is take control out of his hands for a second and he'll be weakened, and if he's weakened, if only for a moment, people will see that and it will make them wonder, even if just a little, if one day there will be a world without Psi."

"That's not what I do," The Guide said.

"I know. You'll threaten him and lose your temper, but that won't get you anywhere. It will make you seem hostile. You know, everyone goes by labels now, as if they're all just one thing. The Troll, The Moderator, The Guide...it's as if you all think you can only play one part."

"If you know so much about it, why don't you do it?" The Guide said.

"I intend on, but I need you with me, because like it or not, right now, you're the face of this, and you need to be smart. You said it yourself: winning isn't going to come from fighting. We need to use our brains."

"Alright," The Guide said, suppressing all anger he would have upon seeing The Moderator's face. "How do we troll him?"

"We just don't care," Iris said. "We make him understand that we can't be beat because we have no interest in anything he has to say..."

"I am letting them sweat while they wait," The Moderator said, sitting cross-legged on the parking garage cement across from The Surfer.

"Why?" The Surfer asked, his voice raspy and weak. He'd lost definition in his face and his eyes were sunken and hidden by strands of hair which hung over his face.

"Power move," The Moderator said. "Always leave them waiting, especially in moments of anxiety."

"You're evil."

"This is just business," The Moderator said. "So tell me about this Guide. Was he your first lieutenant?"

"He's a friend."

"Then, surely you will be distraught when he dies."

"Take me instead."

The Moderator laughed so hard that his neck jerked almost painfully. He recovered quickly. "I find it interesting that you're bargaining, as if you have something to bargain with. As if you have anything I even partially want."

"I'm asking you as a human being."

"That's too bad, because I'm slightly above human Surfer. I've turned a billion people into puppets, so I'm going to go ahead and operate under the assumption that I'm not just one of you." His words came out as almost disgusted when he said 'you' but he couldn't contain it. The Surfer knew he really did see himself as a god—as a puppet master of the people. He would have given anything just to have the chance to take him down a peg, but it seemed The Moderator's power had no limit and it was impossible to reason with him.

"Do you need me to beg?" The Surfer asked. "Is that what you'd like?"

"I'll decide after I talk to The Guide. How's that sound?"

The Surfer closed his eyes. The last thing he wanted was The Guide talking to Moderator. Though he thought highly of his friend, The Guide would likely lose his temper and threaten him. Then, it would be over. He watched The Moderator set up a screen, his eyelids fluttering as he navigated on-line. Then, he set a transmitter down, repositioned the screen so it was directed on his face, and hit 'transmit'.

The world watched the broadcast.

"Good evening," The Moderator said, addressing the cameras instead of his captives. "Tonight we will be discussing and determining the punishments that the terrorists known as Iris and The Guide deserve. As you all know, The Magician is heading the hunt to capture the terrorist known as The Troll, so I will be conducting tonight's interrogation. We will now begin."

The Moderator turned to the screen and took a long look at Iris first. Her hair hung in front of her face as if to conceal her identity. "This is the infamous Iris. Tell me Iris: How do you feel about how your challenge played out?"

Iris wanted to scream, to give him a piece of mind, but she resisted and instead played the game they'd agreed they would play. "We did much better than I expected," she said.

The Moderator was taken aback. He laughed to himself cleverly and leaned toward the screen. "Is getting caught so soon better than expected?"

"My candidate is still out there," she said.

"But we have Rainbow," he shot back.

"We didn't have all our eggs in that basket," Iris said, bluffing carelessly. To her side, The Guide's eyes shifted toward her, slightly amused at what she was trying to do. "I think your downfall will be your confidence and belief that you've thought of everything," Iris added.

"And what haven't I thought of?" he asked, calling her bluff.

She forcefully laughed. "I'd be stupid if I told you," she said. "I may not live to see it, but you're downfall is coming."

The Moderator paused, carefully controlling his movements and facial expressions. He turned to The Guide instead.

The Surfer leaned forward, searching his friend's eyes for any hope that this wasn't over. It made him sad to see The Guide so helpless.

"Guide," The Moderator said. "Where did you come from?"

"I was chosen to watch over The Troll," he said.

"Chosen by who?"

"The leader of the resistance," he said.

"How big is the resistance?"

"I couldn't speak for other chapters, but we're a few thousand strong in the Midwest."

"Oh, please," The Moderator said. "Give me a break. You speak as if you have organization and numbers, but there's no evidence of this other than your words. With thousands in number, we surely would have seen an attack by now."

"I don't really need you to believe me," The Guide said, maintaining all self control. "You're asking questions and I'm answering."

"This is also an interrogation in which your answers could mean the difference between life and death."

The Guide laughed. The Moderator waited silently, but at his side, The Surfer watched in fascination, shocked that his friend was so calm and collected and clearly trying to scare the man.

"You shouldn't insult me or the viewers," The Guide said. "The world isn't actually as dumb as you assume. I think we all know I'm going to die tomorrow. This is just foreplay for you."

"I don't enjoy this any more than you do."

"Again…you're insulting your audience. Of course you're going to kill me. Iris and I have done far too much damage to this game. I understand it was supposed to be simple: You pretend Iris propose a game that you staged at Surfer's trial. You pick a guy who loves Psi and offer him a spot in Chicago if he transmits and betrays the mission, but he never does. Instead, he joins the resistance and kidnaps The Acrobat and brings down a helicopter operated by The Pilot. We spared his life because we're not killers, but I don't blame you for being embarrassed about how things turned out. From your vantage point, killing us before this goes any further makes sense. I'm not even going to try to make a case for myself. But most importantly, when you kill us, and when you killed everyone else, you enjoyed it immensely. You can't even fake sadness well when you talk about how you murdered your daughter and wife."

The Moderator's jaw was down. He couldn't understand how The Guide had learned so much, but he'd also mixed it with false statements. He'd said so much that The Moderator didn't even know where to begin in defending himself. This case would need some major PR later, but all he could do was try to turn the conversation another way.

Iris couldn't help but smile and from off the camera, The Surfer watched proudly as well. The Moderator was at a loss for words. His neck twitched and he gathered his composure. "I don't even know what you are talking about," he said simply. "There was no downed chopper. I never spoke to Iris in my life. I've always been a man of my word and I've proved that time and time again, and I grieved plenty over my family. You don't know what I've been through."

"I'm not sure you're allowed to grieve over people that you yourself needlessly killed," The Guide said.

The Guide understood why they were doing what they were doing. The Moderator was on the defense, a position he wasn't used to. Even if people believed him, somehow the conversation was making him look like a fool. He was backed into a corner.

"That's okay," Iris said, interjecting again. "We would say the same thing if we were you. We don't want innocent people to die, so we are willing to retract our claims if it will save those you intend to murder in the morning."

"Please…" The Moderator said, growing frustrated. "I am punishing the actions of The Troll. Please don't twist my intentions into such a negative light."

"I apologize," Iris said. "I didn't mean to imply that ending the lives of random innocent people was murder. You are right."

The Moderator opened his mouth and closed it again, suddenly aware of what they were doing and eager to end the broadcast. "I see we are not taking this seriously," he said.

"A day from now, we won't be alive," The Guide said. "What would we find important enough to take seriously? If anything, Iris and I were enjoying our conversation until this broadcast. You're wasting the only time we have left on unimportant things."

"Then let's get down to business," The Moderator said. "Because I'm a man of compassion, I will allow you to choose the death you would like."

"You say you're a man of your word?" The Guide said.

"I am."

"I choose a murder suicide by your hands," The Guide said, smiling cleverly.

"I see," The Moderator said, nodding thoughtfully as Iris tried not to laugh. The Surfer was on his feet, aware they'd somehow verbally beaten The Moderator at his own game. "Then I will allow your captors to choose for you." He turned to the camera and addressed the audience with a smile. "Thank you for tuning in," he said. His voice shook unexpectedly before he ended the broadcast.

"He didn't recognize you," The Guide said, quietly.

"I told you he wouldn't."

"Are you angry about that?"

"Leaving me to die along with millions of people is why I'm angry," Iris said.

"Right…"

"It went well," Iris said.

"It was fun. I'll give you that. But in the end, it won't change anything."

"Maybe not, but I like to think that we just exposed a piece of him tonight, that all over the world, people are reminded that he's an evil man. When we die tomorrow, we can die knowing that maybe we helped jump-start the revolution. It's not much, but we have to assume that we've set something in motion."

The Guide nodded with a smile. He watched clouds cover the sky and began to shake as he became suddenly aware of how cold he was.

"The Surfer is very proud of you," Iris said.

"He'll be disappointed at the outcome of all this, but it's no one's fault. This was always uphill. I'm happy I got to fight the good fight and not be killed hiding or running. We faced this. That's going to have to be good enough."

Iris watched the remainder of the sun disappear in the distance. The shape of the bridge began to fade in the dark and the only sound they could hear was the Mississippi in the distance. They'd gotten so close to a waterway. It didn't feel like it should be over yet. "I wish I could see you right now," Iris said.

"Me too," The Guide said softly.

CHAPTER 4

The Troll had about three days of catching up to do to make it to The Guide and Iris. Luckily, The Acrobat and the powers that be at Circular Prime had plenty of luxuries squirreled away to make life easier for themselves.

The Troll had seen each bounty hunter carry a hand-held computer for tracking and communicating. Not long after The Troll and Acrobat set out, The Acrobat retrieved his own device and displayed a map which had small red dots all over the state, each one representing a hidden mode of transportation. The Troll's mind spun. He always knew things like this existed, but to see proof...he wondered if he could have actually gotten somewhere with Rainbow if only he had this knowledge before. There were certainly a lot more modes of transportation than he expected. A quick glance at The Acrobat's map opened a lot of other questions up. There were all kinds of icons and colored areas on the map. It seemed the geography of the land had a few secrets.

There was a bus and a compact car in the vicinity, but they walked an extra five miles so they could grab a couple mopeds. The Acrobat insisted they draw as little attention to themselves as possible, and wanted to stay off the main roads. Another setback occurred when The Acrobat realized The Troll had no idea how to work an automobile and spent the next hour teaching him how to drive, and another two, stopping constantly along the way as the moped kept tipping over. By the time darkness started to fall, The

Troll had a rhythm and was driving along the prairie, the wind in his hair as he kicked up dirt behind. With nothing but time to think and drive, he couldn't help but smile. He was free of the cell, still alive, and driving—which he'd only heard about as a thing of the past.

The Acrobat led the way and The Troll followed, daring himself to trust that The Acrobat wasn't just going to turn him in. Somewhere along the way, there seemed to grow a mutual respect between them. Maybe it was that he spared The Acrobat's life, or that they spent days in a cell together, that The Troll released him, or maybe The Acrobat didn't truly respect The Moderator—that it was a long time coming for him to finally stand up.

But if The Acrobat was anti-Psi...then anyone could be. The Troll allowed himself to rethink Psi again but came up with nothing more than his creed not to fight battles that you can't win and to try to get through life without falling victim of corruption, whether it was The Moderator or in the time before him. The same problems and fears always existed and most of the world tried to navigate around those issues and turn a blind eye when their neighbor fell victim to them. It was normal to want to live, be happy, to simply not fall victim. People like The Surfer were a rarity. The unique individual who didn't fear death or give up when the odds were against them. For The Surfer, it was about principle first and his own life second. The Troll could never accept that creed. The alternative was his own. But what had once seemed impossible had taken The Troll further than he expected and forced him to do things he never thought possible.

The Acrobat's moped skidded to a halt and a cloud of dust puffed up in front of The Troll. He halted abruptly and the moped jumped a little as it came to a stop. He turned to The Acrobat to see why they were stopping and saw he was facing to the left.

"We have time," The Acrobat said. "I want to check something out."

Half an hour later, they pulled into a small town and The Acrobat led The Troll on back roads until they were outside of the town where the land was outstretched for miles of nothingness. It was one large plain, except for a giant circus tent. The Troll stared at the Acrobat as he slowly climbed off the moped, hypnotized by the tent. He walked slowly toward it, without any concern as to whether or not The Troll followed, but he did.

The smell of burnt tires lingered in the air and as they got closer to the tent, The Troll could taste it in his mouth. He followed The Acrobat into what was once presumably a very meaningful place to him. It didn't look like much to The Troll's eyes though. He could only imagine the colors that were once displayed throughout the arena and the smell of popcorn and cotton candy. It was now covered in dirt and dust and everything was tossed on its side or pushed into a corner haphazardly.

The Acrobat wandered slowly to the center, right where he remembered a large net had been. He looked into the air, but there was no tightrope. Only the ladders on each end which he'd once climbed to perform were still there.

He stood in one spot and turned, his arms outstretched as his mind traveled in time to when the applause of the crowd fueled him. A ray of moonlight shining through a tear in the fabric shined on his face and he closed his eyes, as if pretending a spotlight was hitting him.

He opened his eyes and a smile spread across his face. "It's been a long time since I've been to the circus."

"Was it filled with dead people then too?" The Troll asked, nodding toward the stands, where skeletons were draped over chairs.

"This must have been a place where people gathered," The Acrobat said, stepping toward the stands and scanning the crowd of bones. "Unbelievable…"

The Troll watched him with his eyes, relieved The Acrobat was distraught by the sight. He needed him on his side, and the more exposed the world was, the easier it would be.

"What if you help me save Iris and Guide?" The Troll asked.

The Acrobat turned and shook his head. "You say that as if it's a possibility."

"Maybe it is."

"Then describe your plan to me Troll."

The Troll thought, but was stumped. "I don't know. I don't have one, okay?"

"What good is a rescue mission without a plan?"

"The plan is to wing it."

"Sure," The Acrobat said, irritated. "Let's just walk into town where Coach and Mortician are guarding them, with The Pilot overhead and The Moderator with his finger on a button, willing to kill millions of people. Let's wing it. Sounds like a great plan."

"The Pilot will be there?" The Troll asked. "How do you know?"

"He's part of our group. He scares the shit out of everyone. He'll be there if he wants to be, and he'll want to be."

"Did he say that or did he just stare at you? You ever consider that he's just a sissy who figured out how to fool everyone into thinking he's not?"

"If you want to go hand to hand with him, be my guest. I'm helping you turn yourself in. That's it."

"But you *want* to help me, don't you..." The Troll said, as if he'd figured it all out. "You don't approve of anything they're doing."

"Of course I don't!" The Acrobat said, suddenly passionate. "Look around you. How many people have you seen along the way? Everyone's dead or hiding in groups, trying to find their next meal. You know who was among them? My own parents. They're probably among the people in the stands." The Acrobat threw up a hand and scanned the crowd with it. "We expressed concern before he did it. We said people would die. He told us it would be seconds that Psi would shut down, but it was two whole minutes. When that time expired, I wanted to call my parents and siblings. I wanted to rush out and find my friends, but he forbid it. He said we wouldn't be safe out in the world right now. Later, he told me my parents were still alive and well, but one night, about a year later, I'm in his office and he steps out, so I decide to look and see for myself and looked them up in the computer. Both my parents—dead. They died the night Psi froze them. I don't know what they were doing or where they were— just that they died. And he knew that too. I should have known he didn't care. His wife died, he thinks his kid died, and I swear to you Troll: He didn't shed a tear for them."

"Then I don't get why you're not going to help me."

"Because you're talking about a rescue mission to save two people and even if you did pull it off, he'd just kill a few million to get back at you. You can't beat him. The only way to keep the world safe is to keep The Moderator happy, and so that's what we do. We follow orders to keep him happy. And the crazier he gets, the more we bite our tongue."

"But if you all feel this way..."

"I'm the only one left in Circular Prime who feels this way. The others have become so desensitized to it all. People are binary to them. Bar codes. Ones and zeros. For you to end Psi, you would be fighting nine men who individually could easily kill you."

"But we can take the mission back. If we can get Rainbow back and save Guide and..."

"You still need a plan!" The Acrobat shouted. "Without a plan, you've got a fantasy. Fantasies will not restore the world!"

The Troll fell silent and he watched the dust fall in the air like snowflakes and swirl around in the moonlight. He could see The Acrobat wanted to help but couldn't. It reminded The Troll of himself. He hadn't really changed. He'd just realized that there were things that needed to be done. He wished he could be back on the boards, fighting with people and antagonizing them until they snapped. He wished conflict could be less real again.

The Acrobat turned and walked for the exit, passing a cage, what was once a candy stand, a pile of bones which had once belonged to a tiger, a red plastic clown nose. The Troll hurried to catch up with him. The Acrobat walked quickly, as if he wanted to get out of the tent as soon as possible. As they felt the cool breeze in their face, they stopped as screens lit up in the sky. They silently watched the broadcast, their eyes frozen to The Guide and Iris as they turned the conversation against The Moderator.

When it ended, The Troll turned to The Acrobat, who was equally frozen in place. "He denied you took down the chopper," The Acrobat said.

"No one ever accused him of being honest," The Troll said.

"Your friends did a good thing there," The Acrobat said. "He looked flustered."

"They were doing what I do," The Troll said, bitterly. "They don't need me anymore, but they're doing what I do. There's not..." The Troll trailed off and finished quietly, "...my friends."

They hopped on their mopeds and drove the next two hours until they finally came within range of the sound of the Mississippi crashing below. They left the mopeds behind and walked toward the town, and when they were close, they circled at a distance, staying on high ground and among the trees. There was little movement below. There was an occasional passerby, but it was mostly quiet.

The Troll saw them first, bound to the fountain, facing away from each other. It was the only light in the dark and displayed them for everyone to see. He squinted his eyes at them. The Guide and Iris looked dead. He started walking toward them but The Acrobat's arm shot out and grabbed his own.

"You're crazy if you think you can just walk in there."

"Then what do I do?"

"You transmit here and now. Turn yourself in and I'll talk to The Moderator. You probably won't get Chicago, but we might be able to put you back where you started."

"And then what?"

"And then you've saved millions of lives."

"And what happens to them?" The Troll asked, gesturing toward The Guide and Iris.

"I don't see a lot of scenarios that play out where they're not dead in the end."

"Do you see any that do?"

The Acrobat paused. "Troll, you walk down there to save them and you'll be dead before you even reach the fountain and then they're dead too. It's time to do what we came here to do. You need to transmit now."

The Troll pulled the transmitter from his pocket and held it close to his eye, studying it. Transmitting now meant a certain end, but no matter how much he brainstormed, in his head, he came up blank.

"Make up a story," The Acrobat said. "Find a way to stay in The Moderator's good graces and you'll have a fighting chance."

"And how do I do that?"

"When you, me, and Iris were walking, you expressed the reason you troll. Use that. Make something up, outright lie. Smoke and mirrors, remember?"

"Smoke and mirrors," The Troll said, his eyes narrowing as a revelation began to hit him. He tuned the world out as his mind began to spin, and by the time he was done, The Acrobat was staring at him perplexed. "Smoke and mirrors," The Troll said again, with some confidence.

"Yeah, so what?"

"How about I describe my plan now?"

CHAPTER 5

The Pilot flew a small stunt plane in the sky, his every spin calculated. He'd hoped for a sighting of The Troll but wasn't surprised when the early hours of the morning hit and he was a no-show. The Coach and The Mortician woke to the sound of the plane overhead. The Coach forced himself out of bed and shook his head with dissatisfaction. The Pilot was the sharpest, most focused person he knew, and somehow functioned 100% on little or no sleep.

The Mortician stayed in his bed silently for a long time, as if he was getting himself ramped up for the day's events. The Coach was all business as he loaded his duffel bag with six metallic objects and filled his jacket with soft pouches. The Mortician had only heard of his special "skill" but had yet to see it in action. The Coach didn't look like much at first glance, but there was a reason he was called The Coach and the duffel bag held the key.

The Pilot was seemingly bitter. The Mortician though…he only had his own interests in mind: To watch the life drain from someone's eyes was all he lived for. The Coach was there to weaken and taunt them, but The Mortician was allowed the final kiss of death.

The Coach hurried The Mortician along, reminding him that when the sun was in the sky, the time would come to punish The Guide and Iris.

They found The Acrobat on the ground outside the motel, laying with his arm outstretched as if he'd almost completed his journey but fell short. The Coach crouched down and shook him awake, concerned for his well-being while The Mortician stood back and watched with fascination.

The Acrobat turned and blinked his eyes as if coming to. He suddenly sat up. "Water…" he gasped and The Mortician ran off to fetch some water.

"What happened?" The Coach asked. "Did you see The Troll?"

"They locked me up with him," he said, nodding toward The Guide and Iris. "Troll's still there…locked in a cell."

The Coach took in the information, thinking hard about what it meant. It meant one in ten people would die this morning unless someone told The Moderator that The Troll was unable to turn himself in. The Coach didn't see the need to tell though. They could pick up The Troll later and make an example of him. All in all, it would be an eventful morning filled with death and destruction and The Coach could still be back in time for lunch.

When The Acrobat finished his story, The Coach scratched his head and pretended to consider. "Let's keep that to ourselves for now," he said. "We'll finish up here and take care of him later."

"We need to tell The Moderator," The Acrobat said.

"Don't get soft on me Acrobat," The Coach said. "I'm almost positive this is what he wants. If The Troll can't call it off in person, then there's no point. To the public, it will seem as if we bluffed and made up a last minute excuse. Just hang tight and we'll get you some water and something to eat. You've been through a lot. Let's get you to a room."

The Acrobat wanted to protest but bit his tongue. Their plan was far from complete, but he hoped simply placing The Troll in a helpless situation would stop The Moderator from executing millions. Instead, he could only wait and hope that The Troll would come through on his end.

The Coach and Mortician fed The Acrobat and gave him plenty of water, unknowing that he was feigning his weakness. When they were alone in the hotel, The Acrobat went over his story again, which was mostly truth, up until the point The Troll talked him into helping stop The Moderator. It was an easy lie to pull off, but though he appreciated the theory of what The Troll was hoping to pull off, he didn't see it coming together the way The Troll described. The Troll wasn't a fighter, and he needed fighters to win.

The Guide and Iris were fighters though, and without them, The Troll wouldn't win today.

"I want to see The Guide," The Acrobat said, looking up.

"Sorry, but this is our kill," The Coach said.

"I don't care about that," The Acrobat said. "I was locked up for days. I could have starved to death. I have the right to see him before he dies. They left me there."

The Coach stepped aside and gestured for him to go ahead and say whatever last words he had. They all walked into the hall but The Acrobat asked if he could shower first. The Mortician brought him a fresh pair of clothes as he showered and they walked back to the fountain to wait. In the bathroom, The Acrobat smashed the mirror with his elbow and picked out a shard of glass that looked like a long claw. He tucked it into his pants and covered it with his shirt. He was pleased that there was no suspicion raised, and there never would have to be. At the very least though, he could give the resistance a chance. He didn't know why he was going the extra mile for them. He wanted to stop the killing, but had no investment in ending Psi... except...without Psi, The Moderator could never make this threat again. He could never deactivate another person just because he was having a bad day. The Acrobat wasn't willing to fight, but they deserved a shot.

He approached the fountain where The Coach and Mortician stood back and watched as The Acrobat walked a large circle around the fountain. Iris and The Guide were surprised to see him and could only assume the worst.

"What did you do with The Troll?" Iris asked.

"He didn't make it out," he said with a smile.

The Guide was unsurprised, but Iris hung her head, disheartened to hear this.

"You left me there to die," The Acrobat said with a sneer, stepping onto the stone wall that surrounded the water and facing The Guide across the way.

"I left you to kill The Troll," The Guide said. "I was indifferent in what would happen to you."

The Acrobat stepped into the fountain and approached The Guide, standing face to face. He suddenly balled up his fist and hit him in the stomach, knocking the wind out of The Guide. The Coach laughed from the side.

The Acrobat stood nose to nose with The Guide and before The Guide could spew off a threat, he said, "There will be a signal."

The Guide felt something sharp slip into his hand, out of range from where The Coach and Mortician could see.

"What?" The Guide asked, searching Acrobat's eyes, trying to find the bluff or a trick.

"You'll know when," The Acrobat said. "Trust me. It will be hard to miss."

With that, he turned and left the fountain, approaching The Coach and Mortician with a laugh and buddying up to them again. The Guide's brain worked a mile a minute, trying to decipher what could possibly be happening. The Acrobat was with them? There was only one way that was possible: The Troll. They'd certainly had time to spend together, but what happened in that time? A fraction of hope filled him as he considered the possibilities. In his hand was an escape option: A shard of glass he could use to work through the rope. There was also the possibility of an attack of some sort, but by...The Troll? What could he possibly do?

And when? There was only moments left to strike if it was really going to happen. He watched The Acrobat hurry back to the hotel, as if trying to get away from the scene. His eyes darted from one spot to the next, searching for a clue as to what was about to happen.

But nothing did. The only movement was the stunt plane in the sky, whirring by every few moments.

Business went on as promised and The Coach and Mortician approached the fountain with sinister smiles on their faces.

"You really angered The Moderator with your last broadcast," The Coach said.

"Good," The Guide said without hesitation.

"What is it that makes you so stubborn? It's as if you have no concern at all for your own well being, even when you're in a war you can't win."

"That's the difference between us," The Guide said. "I'm a man of principle. You're just a sheep...afraid that if he cares about something, someone will hurt him. A hundred years from now, we're both going to be dead Coach. You're just going to die a coward."

"Everyone has a weakness though," The Coach said as he circled slowly around the fountain to where Iris was bound.

"Talk to *me*," The Guide said, trying to carry the conversation. The Coach ignored him and came face to face with Iris, his eyes full of fire as he considered the task ahead of him.

"You'll be last," The Coach said. "I'd like you to hear this."

The Guide tried talking to The Mortician. He screamed. He begged. It all fell on deaf ears though as he listened to The Coach as he began taunting Iris, running his hands over her face and down her shoulders and hips. The Guide was ready to cut his ropes, but held on a little longer. If he broke out now, he'd still have The Coach, Mortician, AND Pilot to face. Any anger he felt, he would contain as long as possible until there was a signal.

A damn signal. His mind spun as Iris sobbed. He heard the plane circle in the sky. The sounds all blended together, piercing his ears as he tore apart inside, completely helpless to circumstance. "You don't have to do it this way!" he shouted, but whatever The Coach was doing, he didn't stop. "Damn-it Troll!" The Guide shouted, and finally, The Coach did stop, and circled back to face him.

"Troll?" The Coach asked. "Your Troll was nothing but a gimmick to show the world that no one cares for your cause Guide. He didn't even make it out of state, and where is he now?"

"Coach…" The Mortician said, distracted by something in the distance. The Coach turned and saw The Mortician was looking toward the bridge. He followed Mortician's eyes to where the silhouette of a man stood in the center, looking out toward the plane, as if to face The Pilot. The Coach squinted his eyes and stepped forward, trying to get a better view.

As The Coach and Mortician tried to make sense of what they were seeing, The Guide readied his shard of glass. He'd know the signal when it came, but he wondered what The Troll possibly could do alone on a bridge against The Pilot. Was this the signal? If so, it wasn't what The Acrobat was making it out to be. Or maybe The Acrobat really wasn't trying to help. Maybe this was more trickery. He started to slowly cut at his ropes.

The Troll stood watching the stunt plane as it circled the sky twice, as if The Pilot was trying to decide if he was really standing there. What The Pilot was supposed to see was a strong confident Troll challenging him, but what he couldn't see was how his hands were shaking, his knees were weak, and a weight in his chest made it impossible for him to swallow.

The timing was key, and for a focused opponent like The Pilot, it would take a great distraction to cause him to falter, a great distraction to beat him. What he needed The Pilot to do was something he never did: Flinch. And if he could pull it off and if The Acrobat came through on his end, and if The Guide and Iris could free themselves and get away with Rainbow, they could all recommit to their journey—if they would have him.

The stunt plane passed over his head and put some distance between it and the bridge before making a wide loop and positioning itself in line with the bridge. From the distance, Iris watched in fascination as The Troll was seemingly committing suicide in front of her eyes. But suicide wasn't in his nature, and unless The Troll believed this was something he could handle, she couldn't understand why he was even here at all. Unless she'd misjudged him and her initial opinion was right: The Troll refused to lose: Online, in person, against the odds…The Troll wanted to win. Except there was no way he could win that she could see. She wondered if he had a trick up his sleeve, or if this was just a ploy to rally her. She tugged at her ropes, but she was bound tightly and her wrists burned from having pulled at her ropes all night long. Without a miracle, this was the end, even if The Troll volunteered himself to die along with them. She watched and waited.

The Troll readied himself as the stunt plane faced his direction, coming faster at him than he had time to react. He was ready to execute the plan, but The Pilot was flying too high. The timing was off on this round. If he was shot, it was all for nothing. He ran to the side as bullets began hitting the pavement and sending concrete in the air with poofs of smoke all around him. The engine above him roared and the plane passed overhead. He surveyed his body and found no blood.

Round two, he thought and carried himself a few feet from where a path of bullets tore at the pavement to give The Pilot a better view. He wrapped his fingers tightly around the transmitter and touched his inner pocket to make sure his weapon was intact. He was relieved it was there and even more relieved as the sun began to rise in the sky. He had a feeling all eyes were on him and that The Moderator hadn't executed anyone yet…as if every plan was in limbo and the clock stopped all around, waiting for his death before the world could continue to rotate again.

The plane made a wide loop, putting more distance between it and the bridge. The Troll forced himself to breath steadily, reminding himself he was going to have one chance at this. The Pilot fired from farther away this time, at a greater speed. He flew lower but by The Troll's calculations, it wasn't low enough. This time, he wasn't sure he could outrun the bullets because they constantly sent sparks and pavement flying up around him. Instead he ducked behind a metal beam, trying to get a grasp on his weapon but failing as the plane approached, gunfire spattering faster and harder all around him, blinding and deafening him as he cradled himself as close to the beam as possible until the engines passed overhead.

That was it. He knew he wouldn't survive a third pass and he wasn't sure the bridge would either. His body had loosened and adrenaline pumped through him as he realized the fear of death was gone and he was in full mission mode, as focused as The Pilot—maybe more. Wasn't that really what this was? A staring contest? A jousting competition between man and machine, or man and machine within machine? The Pilot was a more than worthy opponent, but The Troll thought back to Iris telling him that the world was taken with brains—not weapons, and it would have to be taken back the same way.

Round three.

The Troll spun toward where The Pilot looped his plane back and repositioned, flying lower—flying as low as The Troll needed him to fly. He reached in his inner pocket and flipped the transmitter on, where all over the world monitors flashed on and people turned to see what The Moderator was broadcasting this time. But this time, they instead saw The Troll with a determined look in his eyes, holding the transmitter at his side, not using it to send a message but instead using it as a weapon. He looked into the sky where a hundred screens displayed the ground where the transmitter's camera was aimed.

The plane was flying fast, but it didn't fire. The Troll saw the guns slowly turning as if they were zoning in on his body. He was very likely seconds away from death, but everything looked as it should and he closed his eyes for a moment and whispered to himself: *You can beat him.*

From his inner pocket he pulled a mirror. He held it to the

camera and triangulated it with the sun. All at once, the world around him went white and sunlight bounced off every surface.

The Pilot never knew what happened, and every instinct inside told him to keep moving in a straight line, aim the guns, eliminate the target...but none of those things were possible. He no longer could see the bridge, or The Troll, and the last thing he knew, he was flying right at it, avoidable only by pulling away. In the moments of confusion, his timing was lost and his thoughts were too prolonged to believe it possible. He jerked the handles to the side, immediately feeling the shame in losing his focus. The plane started to arc, but everywhere it turned, the blinding of sunlight bouncing from screen to screen only caused him to lose his sense of direction.

He tried to bring the plane below it, but there were monitors everywhere and it was unavoidable. And then, he didn't know which direction he was flying—north, south...he had no idea. He turned to his instruments as a guide, but all he could realize was that his altitude was low and whatever direction he was moving didn't matter, because eventually...

And then the wing snapped off and the plane began to spin. The last thing he saw before impact was the bridge, and the plane around him shattered.

As The Troll's eyes went wide, surprisingly shocked by his success, he pulled the camera away and focused on the ruined plane instead. The helicopter crash was clearly covered up, but this was unavoidable. The world was undoubtedly watching, and now they truly would see that the men in Circular Prime could be beat—even the best of them. He walked toward the wreckage with a smile, but it faded quickly as a foot kicked a piece of shrapnel away and The Pilot began to roll out.

The Troll set his weapons on the pavement and considered running, but waited instead. The Pilot had always been a pain in his ass, even without having said a word. He decided this was a fight he was going to stick around for.

The Guide never knew what happened or why it happened, but he heard the crash and the blinding light around him was most definitely the signal The Acrobat had warned him about. He wasted no time severing the ropes once it happened, and when he fell to the water below, he looked around and saw no one was coming. No one could make out anything that was happening, but The Guide could easily find his way around the statue to where Iris was bound. Within seconds, he cut her down and found her hand. They made their way out of the fountain and started running. Their feet were still wet and cold and tingled from being bound so long. They pushed forward with little feeling and little vision, but knew they were running in the opposite direction of where they'd last seen The Coach and Mortician.

As The Guide began to wonder how long the distraction would last, it suddenly disappeared and the world around them normalized. He turned back and saw they'd put a good distance between themselves and The Coach and Mortician and when the lights turned off, their enemies' attention was focused toward the bridge, so they ran until they disappeared behind a building and kept going.

"We won't have much time," The Guide said. "They're going to figure out where we are."

"They still have Rainbow," Iris said. "We have to get it back or they'll destroy it."

"Did you see if either of them had a gun or any kind of weapon?"

"I don't think so. I didn't see anything. The Coach has a duffel bag which he calls "his players" but I'm not sure what that means."

"Are you okay?" The Guide asked, finding her eyes. She shook her head and fell into his arms as he wrapped around her in a hug. She clung to his body, digging her fingers into his shoulders from behind. "I'm going back for Rainbow," he said over her shoulder.

"I'm going too."

"No," he said. "If we all die, there's nothing left to stop them. The world needs someone to rally people, and you're good at that. So is The Troll. This is what I do."

"But…"

"You circle back to the bridge and see if he's okay. If I can get Rainbow, I'll join you on the other side. We need to eliminate some of their guys so the world knows we're a real army. I can do that."

"Promise me you'll meet us down there," she said, finding his eyes again.

"I'll do everything I can."

The Guide wanted to kiss her, but there was no time. It gave him more incentive to survive, but he wasn't sure what he was up against. The bounty hunters supposedly all had skills. Some were known, such as The Mentalist or Chameleon, but others were tucked away. The Guide understood who The Mortician and The Coach were, but he didn't understand what they could do, though he had the feeling he'd find out very quickly. He'd have a hard enough time fighting two against one.

He wanted to see Iris again. He wanted to recover the Rainbow and save the world. He wanted to defeat an enemy like The Troll had. At the precinct, he'd told The Troll that he took down a helicopter and asked The Troll what he'd ever done. Supposedly, The Troll was all about one-upping, but if The Pilot was out of the picture, the game was on. Killing two more bounty hunters and hitting the road would be just the type of act that if the world saw, could create ripples.

He watched Iris protectively as she made a wide circle toward the bridge. Before long, she would move far enough that Coach and Mortician would notice her. It was now or never. He moved fast, emerging from behind the building and running toward the fountain, tightening his body and preparing himself for the most important fight of his life. As The Coach and Mortician were closer in his sights, he could see they had realized The Guide and Iris had escaped and he could see the wreckage below. The odds were swinging back toward The Guide, but this moment would determine everything.

The Coach was closer, and stood against the base of the fountain. He saw him look up and notice The Guide barreling toward him at full speed without enough time to react. He dived in the air and wrapped his arms around The Coach's midsection, sending both of their bodies into the water.

CHAPTER 6

The Pilot and The Troll circled each other, both searching for an opportunity to lunge at the other. The Troll suspected he was right to believe The Pilot wasn't really a fighter and used silence and machinery for intimidation. His eyes were hidden behind his sunglasses, which could easily cover any fear he had and he surely must have some. Twice his aircraft had been taken down and now he was left with what amounted to a bar brawl on his hands.

The Troll had been in a fight or two, but never by his choice. His tongue got him into trouble and sometimes fists were thrown at him, but mostly it would result in a tussle on the ground until both fighters were breathless and tired. This was different though. This would have to be to the death. On either side of the road was the edge of the bridge and The Troll knew that was his only winning scenario. He couldn't pummel The Pilot with punches. He could only force him over the edge.

He thought maybe The Guide would show up, but for some reason he couldn't understand, he wanted this fight. He had a chance if he could catch The Pilot off guard though—if he could cause him to lose his focus.

"You might as well speak at this point," The Troll said. "You've exposed you're not as cool as you try to be when you crashed your plane."

The Pilot's face didn't move. Instead, he swung an arm out, but The Troll leaned back and The Pilot only hit air.

Wear him down, The Troll thought. I'm not a fighter but I erode people's souls until they're too angry, too tired, too exhausted to fight. That's verbal, but does the same work when it's physical?

"Maybe we should figure this out another way," The Troll said, backing away. "We both know your moderator isn't going to be happy with your performance here today."

The Pilot swung again, and this punch connected, but when The Troll tried to dodge it, he managed to put his shoulder in front of him. The punch connected, and it stung, but The Pilot put everything he had in it and was slow to recover. Before The Troll could reposition, The Pilot started to lash out, throwing fists at him from every direction. Some missed, but most hit, and even as he felt the stinging pain hitting him over and over, he could see that The Pilot really wasn't a fighter. He was sloppy with his swings. He would have celebrated the fact if not for the constant pain. Finally, he fell to the ground and covered himself, rolling away as quickly as he could. When he finally was a few feet away, he pushed himself to his feet and told himself that this was just a battle between two inexperienced fighters…that the least awful of them would rise above.

He stepped forward and guarded his face, ready to fight, but mindful of the fact that The Pilot likely had less energy. He wanted to fight, but he wanted to break him down, little by little, until one good shove would send him to the water below. He needed The Pilot to throw the punches and he needed most of them to miss but all of his own to hit. This wasn't a fight of strength. It was a mathematical game.

"Oh my gosh Pilot. Were you hitting me or is there a draft out here?"

The Pilot didn't flinch, but The Troll knew he had to be angry. He was coming at him faster, with more aggression, and The Troll found it wasn't easy to punch a person, but it was easy to dodge someone who used emotion to fight. He sidestepped as The Pilot swung hard, and paused as if catching his breath.

"I was almost your dad you know," The Troll said. "But the guy ahead in line had exact change."

The Pilot spun and backhanded The Troll. It was the best connection he made yet and the sound of flesh on flesh made a loud slap that sent The Troll backward and almost off his feet.

"When I beat you, and people ask about you, I'm going to say you cried and begged for your life," The Troll said. "I'm going to say you wouldn't stop talking."

The Pilot came at him again, as if to tackle him. In that moment, The Troll could see his whole body weight barreling toward him. He backed up quickly and The Pilot lost his footing. He didn't fall, but he fell forward for a moment before regaining himself.

The Pilot tried to move closer, but The Troll blocked him with his arms, keeping him at length. Instead, The Pilot threw another punch that connected, right in the side of the head, causing a shooting pain. This time, his vision went fuzzy and he spun and stepped on a piece of the plane's shrapnel, which slid under his feet and sent him to the ground. His ass hit the pavement hard, and he swore to himself, knowing that punch could be the one that ended the fight.

Then, before he could recover, The Pilot came down on him with full force.

Iris could see the fight on the bridge. It seemed strange to her that The Troll was fighting at all, but as she got closer, she could see he was losing. If he could hang on until she got there, they could team up and take The Pilot down together.

She ran through the streets, only turning back to see that The Guide was in the fountain and had The Coach pinned under the water. He was strong, but she hoped he'd be able to fight both. She hoped he hadn't underestimated who he was fighting. He'd told her to help The Troll, but she felt as if she was choosing between them, and she felt that The Troll was valuable. She hated believing that, since The Guide had been loyal and had always fought for the take-down of Psi, and The Troll had only proved unreliable and untrustworthy.

She picked up the pace and as the bridge became clearer, she could see that the plane had tore up the pavement straight down the middle in large chunks. She could see pieces were shifting all around The Troll and Pilot, but they carried on and so did she.

As she reached the foot of the bridge, she caught movement out of the corner of her eye and her breath stopped in her throat as she recognized the face of one of the men at the bounty hunter dinner.

"Oh, endurance!" The Poet shouted with a smile. "Why is the cold wind at your back?"

She stopped and fixated on him. He stood still, as if to let her pass, but she knew if she tried to keep moving, he would stop her. "I'm helping The Troll," she said.

"You might want to rethink that plan," The Poet said. Iris turned to see he was holding Rainbow. "If you walk away from me, I will destroy this."

The Guide held The Coach underwater with all his force. The Coach seemed to be the stronger of the two and if he could eliminate him quickly, The Mortician would be a piece of cake. Water splashed as The Coach reached for air, thrashing in the water as he used every bit of energy from every part of his body to find air. The Guide tried to find The Mortician out of the corner of his eye, but saw no movement. Instead, he focused on using his strength to drown Coach quickly and assumed The Mortician was hanging back, too afraid to jump in.

Suddenly, a hand wrapped around the back of his neck. It didn't squeeze, but the touch was cold and sent shocks into The Guide's body which started at the touch, but slowly spread, paralyzing him. In that moment, he realized that The Mortician had a weapon. He was a man obsessed with death, and was wired to rot whatever he touched. The Guide could feel his skin and muscles numbing under his touch and could feel the spread of whatever poison was inside him.

The Coach gasped for air as he came up from under the water and standing between them, his legs about to give way, The Guide closed his eyes, feeling defeat.

Then, The Mortician deliberately let go. The Guide fell into the water and the numbness of his body slowly dissipated.

As The Coach was still catching his breath, he grabbed The Guide by the collar and tossed him over the stone foundation. The Guide crashed into the ground, sending pain through his midsection, and rolled away. As his rolling slowed, he forced himself to keep going anyway, putting as much distance between himself and the bounty hunters as he could. Finally, he rolled and pushed off the ground with his hand, jumping to his feet in one swift motion. He turned, where he found himself facing both men at a distance.

The Coach stepped forward. "You're in over your head Guide. That was real dumb what your friend did. I was going to make it easy on you."

"You have the disadvantage," The Guide said. "Iris and Troll are long gone."

"If that were even true, we'd catch them. This game was never designed to be won."

"Then how about we keep this between us?" The Guide said, motioning for them to come at him. "I'll take you both."

"I'm afraid not," The Coach said, walking forward and reaching into his jacket. He came out with a gray pouch which looked like a high tech water balloon. "I'm not a player. I'm a Coach. So catch!"

He tossed the pouch, which arched in the air quickly and came down toward The Guide. If The Guide had more time to think about it, he might have dodged it, but it looked harmless—like something he could throw right back at him. Instead, just as a water balloon would, it burst open on impact and the liquid inside spattered all over The Guide's chest and arms.

He stared at the liquid, which was thicker than water and had a metallic glow to it. "What the hell is this?" he asked, noting it didn't hurt or sting, or have any effect.

"That is what my players use to track."

"Players," The Guide said, slowly.

Suddenly, The Coach's duffel bag opened and scraps of metal emerged and fell together, forming larger and larger masses, bouncing off each other and clinking as the scrap assembled into shapes that were clearly forming the resemblance of a human torso and arms, but no more. Six bodies were brought together and as the finishing touches united on their large metallic torsos, they began to turn and move toward The Guide.

"You've got the ball," The Coach said. "A liquid magnetic gel that serves as a guidance system for my players. They will not stop moving until they've consumed it and anything attached to it."

The players continued to move toward The Guide, picking up pace and readying their long arms. If they caught him, he didn't know what they could possibly do, other than batter him with their large frames. There was no way he could escape, other than to get the gel off his body. He turned and ran and felt the pace of the players pick up on his tail. The Mortician and Coach followed at a slower pace, confident that the players would put him down so they could finish him off.

One of the players hit the back of The Guide's shoulder and spun, tearing a sharp edge across his skin and causing a spurt of blood to trickle down his back. He ran faster, running to the side and edging his way to where it wasn't so open—somewhere he could find something to use against them. Even if that happened, he still had two bounty hunters on his tail.

From a distance, he spotted a scrap-yard and headed for the factory beyond it.

The heat of the fire burned The Troll's eyes as he stepped around the plane, carefully placing his steps to stay upright and balanced. He circled the wreckage slowly as The Pilot followed at a steady walk, as if he didn't feel any urgency. In The Pilot's head, The Troll had no chance, and The Troll knew his only chance was to use that confidence to allow himself to be underestimated.

To beat The Pilot, it would take a little more courage on his part. He evaluated the situation. The Pilot would inevitably catch and kill him unless he caught The Pilot off guard first. All around him, the pavement was cracking and the fire from the plane was melting the asphalt. If they stood in one place, the whole bridge would eventually collapse and kill them both. At the very least, The Troll would take that over his own death and The Pilot walking away a victor.

The Pilot's features didn't move. Behind his sunglasses, his eyes were fixated on his target. The Troll wasn't a fighter. If he did happen to throw a punch or two, they would be weak and not enough to catch The Pilot off guard. He certainly couldn't beat him to death like The Pilot clearly could to him. There was one end to this and it ended with The Pilot in the river below.

The Troll searched the ground for an opening and spotted one that was uncomfortably close to the plane. Under the left wing, a crevice had formed and the ground was continually crumbling with bits of cement and rock breaking away and hitting the steel beams that held up the bridge before tumbling into the water below. The opening was enough to fit through, as long as The Troll could move quickly before the whole area was covered with heat and flames.

He looked up to see The Pilot coming at him faster.

"How about you give me another shot?" The Troll said. "I wasn't really playing the game before, but I will now. What fun is this for you if I'm just caught and killed like this?"

The Troll kept moving toward the broken ground and The Pilot kept walking without response.

"Isn't the thrill of the hunt supposed to be more of a...thrill? Don't you want an opponent who genuinely wants to beat you? I needed some time to get on board. I'm there now. Let's start over."

The Pilot kept coming. The Troll stood against the wing, the broken propeller at his back. He could feel the ground below him where the cement was busted.

"Alright," The Troll said. "If you want to finish this now, we'll finish this now."

The Troll quickly fell to his stomach and rolled under the plane and slipped through the opening.

The Pilot stopped, his expression never changing, and stared at the opening. After a moment, he followed.

Fifty yards to her left, The Troll disappeared from Iris's view. Far up the street to her right, The Guide was long gone as well. She was only left to contend with The Poet, and deep down, she knew that was what she was supposed to do. Rainbow had been her obsession ever since she learned of it's existence. She would never have believed that she'd ever be so close and that the only thing that stood between her and it would be The Poet. It was...actually quite poetic.

He was the weaker of the bounty hunters in her eyes. Usually, they carried some kind of strange gadget or built in super-power, but The Poet seemed to just be a hateful man who owned a persona.

She once again turned both ways, but her friends were gone; maybe defeated. She hoped not, but if they were, she still had a mission and if The Poet were gone, the coast would be clear. She could cross the river and start a new journey with the end of Psi in hand.

The Poet was built well. He stood six foot two inches with curly blond locks that were well tended to. His smile was fake, but well-practiced and pleasant to someone who didn't know any better. He wore what looked like blue Victorian-style garments and usually stood in some kind of pose: akimbo or with a hand on his hip and an index finger on his chin. He was the personification of his name, and though he seemed harmless upon appearance, what really scared Iris was just how confidently he approached.

"My flower," he said. "You are far too delicate to fight. What say you and I come to a truce?"

"Okay," she said, her back turned to The Poet. "How about we…" In a flash, she spun and shot out her heel, kicking him square on the arm. Rainbow flipped over his shoulder and landed on the ground behind him. He was already surprised, and further hesitated as he struggled between going after Rainbow or Iris. In those moments, Iris took the opportunity and moved in on him, throwing punches, all landing on The Poet and catching him off guard. He stepped away, trying to gain some footing, but every punch sent him further off balance until he landed on the ground and winced in pain.

Iris reached out and grabbed Rainbow but The Poet recovered fast and hurried toward her, grabbing around her body and diving to the ground with her in his arms. They landed on top of Rainbow and Iris could feel it under her leg.

She realized her arms were wrapped tightly in his and he held her there, flexing to tighten the grip. She tried to move but realized she was losing feeling. "Let. Me. Go!" she yelled through deep breaths, but he held tighter, expertly squeezing the wind out of her. She tried to head-butt him but couldn't find the energy. She realized that they had escaped an impossible situation only to be defeated moments later. This couldn't be the end.

She couldn't allow it, but she couldn't overpower him. All she could do was fake dead or…

She suddenly leaned in and kissed him, hard and deep. It threw him off guard and his grip loosened but not enough. He pulled back. "I'm not falling for…"

She leaned in and kissed him again and though he would never fall for the trick, it was enough to loosen the grip further. She had a split second before he would regain his grip. Instead of pulling away as he'd expect from her, she moved her body upward, shot her knee between his legs and hit him with everything she had.

His grip let up completely and the look on his face told her that he wouldn't be on his feet anytime soon. She rolled away but quickly turned back to grab Rainbow. Though The Poet wouldn't be able to fight, he knew there was one thing he could do. With one hand, he covered his privies to protect them from further harm, but the other fell over Rainbow and he wrapped his fingers around it protectively.

"Let it go or I'll do it again," she said.

His eyes went wide at the suggestion and he backed away from her, toward the edge of the bridge. She tried to find an angle of attack but he was a toss away from sending the memory stick over the edge and ending their quest forever. Though she'd crippled the man, he owned the advantage.

She came to a halt and froze, hoping he would do the same. She wished she'd moved faster, or hit him twice.

"If you throw that over, I will kill you," she said.

He held his hand at the edge and looked back at her with fear and pain in his eyes. "Stand back," he said.

She stepped backward slowly, keeping her eye on his hand as he allowed himself to recover. "You don't want to drop that," she said.

"And you want to stand back!" he shouted. His pain had warped into anger. "Walk to the opposite side of the bridge!"

She reluctantly complied and found herself facing him from the other end of the street. He repositioned himself and held his hand farther off the bridge. She almost stepped forward, but he shot her a look as if to say 'don't you dare'.

"What do we do about this?" she asked, afraid he'd give the answer she thought he might.

"You're going to jump," The Poet said. "Or this is gone forever."

The Guide entered the warehouse with the robots on his tail. Each player was full of sharp edges and blunt surfaces. If they descended on him at once, he'd be a goner, but The Guide had only one ray of hope left: They were trying to thrill kill him. They were hunting because they didn't want him to be killed by the players. They wanted The Mortician to put his hands on him and suck the life out of him slowly.

The bots were exhausting though. With each nudge, they cut or bruised him and he hadn't even gotten a chance to fight yet. He was limping and sweating and outrageously outnumbered. As badly as he wanted to go after The Coach and Mortician, he had to lose the bots first. He tried to wipe away the metallic gel but only succeeded in smearing it into his skin and clothes. He'd ripped off his shirt and tossed it aside, which distracted a few of the bots, but the remainder followed the scent stuck to him.

The factory was a clutter mess of cages, chains, metal stairs, and a caged elevator in the center, which was suspended by chains and pulleys. He searched the walls for a fire alarm, but the building was long abandoned and not even close to being up to code. He could see the sprinkler system attached to pipes that ran the length of the brick walls and up across the ceiling, which was four stories up. If he were on the fourth floor, he could bust a pipe and wash the gel off his body. He started for the elevator, but from the opposite end of the building, The Mortician entered and began walking toward him, putting himself between the elevator and The Guide.

Instead, he ran for a spiral staircase, only making it a few feet before one of the bots put a sharp edge through his shin. Blood began to stream as he pushed himself up with his arms and began running with most of the weight on his other foot.

The Mortician was in the elevator, pushing a button at a time to follow the floor that The Guide was on.

"Dammit," he muttered. He ascended the stairs, and watched the elevator, seeing The Mortician's eyes glued to him as he worked his way to the top of the factory. Below, at the foot of the steps, The Coach began climbing, two bots orbiting his body as he moved.

A third bot suddenly hovered past The Guide's feet below and up around the stairs, and suddenly zooming by at The Guide's feet, it's full weight hitting his hip and knocking him to his side. He caught a look at The Coach's face as he fell to the nearest platform and wincing as his body hit the metal links that made up the surface. Somehow, the bots were programmed to move like a team, following formations and working in sync of each other.

"Why not a fair fight!?" he yelled, but his voice only echoed in the factory without response.

He pulled himself to his feet and watched as bots hovered at either side, but sat waiting, inviting him to keep moving so they could tease him later with an unexpected strike. He knew he wouldn't make it to the top. He tried to swipe some gel to the ground to throw them off, but there was nothing remaining. He tried to use his sweat to rid himself of the gel, but it did very little for his cause. Every time he smeared a mixture of sweat and gel on a railing, the bots would stop for just a second before moving toward him again.

He carried on, hurrying to the stairs again, but a floor above, the elevator was stopped and The Mortician stepped outside the doors and began walking in his direction. He picked up his pace until he was on the same floor and began sprinting. *Mind over matter*, he told himself as he made a wide circle around The Mortician to dodge his touch. The Mortician only walked, following his direction. The Guide wanted to be in the elevator, but The Mortician guarded the door with his body, keeping close to it but following The Guide as he tried to maneuver around him. He was finally back at the stairs and welcome to move up, but as The Mortician got into the elevator, he quickly switched his plan and stayed on that floor. He had little time before The Mortician would switch the direction of the elevator. He ran for it, grabbing a metal rod on the way and just as the elevator stopped on that floor, he wedged the rod between both doors. In that moment, The Mortician reached out and their hands touched, but The Guide pulled away and fell to the ground, rattling the metal below him.

The Mortician reached for the rod but it was out of his grasp. The Guide ran for the stairs again, ducking as one of the bots came close to hitting him in the side of the head. It spun past and stopped in mid air and began to follow him slowly again. He made an inventory of the warehouse, searching for bots, and discovered they were all hovering near him—any one of them could suddenly move in his direction and batter him.

The Coach was nearing his floor as he began moving to the next. Without The Mortician to stop him, he could burst a pipe and get the bots off his tail, but he would still have the bounty hunters to contend with and his energy was low.

A bot was suddenly in his face, blocking his entry to the fourth floor. Instead of ducking or dodging, he wrapped his arms around the metal and ran forward with it in his arms, sharp edges of the bot digging into his skin as he hugged it tightly. He reached the fourth floor just as the elevator was almost to the top. He tossed the bot above the elevator and watched with satisfaction as it was crushed between the wheels and elevator as it reached the top.

The Guide was on the top floor, facing The Mortician, who started to work his hands through the elevator again for the rod. If he couldn't pry it out, The Coach would. He tried to develop a plan, but barely had the energy to move. He dragged his feet to the wall where a pipe and faucet hung, five feet away. He gasped for breath as he tried to move forward, but his body was caught on bots—bots that held him in place. They surrounded his feet and two placed themselves in front of his chest. The Guide prepared himself for death, traumatized that he'd gotten so close to ridding himself of the bots. The bots slowly turned him as The Coach reached the top, seemingly winded from the stairs himself. It was no wonder The Coach was part of the group. He didn't have to fight. He had his team do it for him.

He faced The Coach, bots holding him in place. Behind his back, The Mortician stood in the elevator, waiting for The Guide to be delivered.

The Coach wore a smug smile. "You're dead Guide. You get that, right?"

"Yeah, I get it," The Guide said. "This is the peace you boys at Circular Prime are always bragging about. This is your non-violent world."

"Oh no," The Coach said. "You've got it all wrong. We reserve violence only for those who don't comply. You shouldn't have stirred the pot."

"Then just finish this."

The Coach said nothing. He just nodded in agreement and activated his bots again. They slowly directed The Guide backwards, right to where The Mortician's arms were reaching out of the elevator.

The Troll stood on a large metal beam, which was one among many beams that criss-crossed under the bridge, reinforcing its strength. It was a long fall to the water below, and above, the bridge blocked out daylight, which only reflected on the water below. Everything under the bridge was silhouettes. The beams below and to his sides were all just shadows, making it harder to maneuver without losing his footing and falling to the water below.

The only light at the end of this tunnel was that The Pilot would face the same problems. The Pilot's shtick wasn't the one The Troll needed right now. He needed to face someone who was afraid as he was to be balancing himself in the dark. The Pilot wouldn't flinch. He wondered if that was a good thing. The Pilot was too busy staying in character to realize when he was in over his head. Crashing his ride was proof that the man could be distracted. But The Troll had no element of surprise left.

He ducked behind a large beam as he saw The Pilot lower

himself into the opening in the street. Chunks of the street fell with him and cascaded to the river below, but The Pilot landed on his feet, causing an echoing clang. He put his arms out for balance, faltered for a moment, but stood straight a moment later and surveyed the area. The Troll could see his silhouette from where he was crouched, but The Pilot would have to come closer to see him, especially since the sunglasses never left his face. He carried on in the dark, so unafraid that darkening the world more wasn't enough deterrent to break character.

The Troll watched, mindful of his upper-hand. If he could manage not to be seen until The Pilot was close enough to give a good shove, he would win. Somehow, he didn't believe that would happen, and if he waited for that instead of acting, he'd be dead.

He'd constantly felt as if his world was turned on its head. The whole last week was too surreal to process. Was the same guy crouched in the dark the same person who not ten days ago prioritized bothering people? His environment had changed and he'd changed too, but without choice. Something was different though. He didn't want to beg for his life and he didn't want to necessarily find his way to Chicago to live among the men at Circular Prime.

All he could think about was defeating The Pilot, and when that was done, he wanted Rainbow, and to show The Guide he wasn't so bad, and to see Iris and make sure she was okay. For all he knew, they were all dead and Rainbow was as good as gone, but if he had to be forced on this journey, he wasn't going to walk away without some kind of trophy. If no other damage was done, he wanted to at least rub it in everyone's face that this smug bastard couldn't get the best of him.

His fingers started moving, but not because he had something to say. He only told himself over and over that he couldn't fall, that he had to focus. He shadow-typed "focus" repeatedly, using it as his only motivation. The feel of the keyboard wasn't there, but he'd spent so much time with it, that he knew how to keep his hands steady. Shadow-typing was his balance beam and hopefully it was better than whatever it was The Pilot had.

He slowly stood, and backed away down a beam, holding a cable in his right hand and moving backward just by feel.

"I think I called it at dinner that night," The Troll spoke loudly, causing The Pilot to turn in his direction and freeze, as if he was trying to figure out what The Troll was up to. "I think you use silence as intimidation, but I have yet to see what you can do. Fighting me isn't an accomplishment. I'm not a fighter, and you knew that from the start. You could have showed up wearing a pink tutu and I would have run from you, but that's the thing Pilot. I'm not going to run. I wouldn't be able to if I tried. I'm going to test this theory and see if you're actually everything you try so hard to personify, or if a vidiot like me can beat you."

The Troll could still only see the shape of The Pilot, but he stood still long enough to make The Troll believe he was faltering. Whatever he was doing, it lacked his usual confidence.

"You know what the problem is Pilot?" The Troll went on, backing up as The Pilot started moving forward. "I've known from the beginning that I wouldn't make this journey. I didn't expect to. None of you thought I'd do as much damage as I've done, and when I'm dead, you're all going to have to explain that. The world saw your plane go down. You can't hide it this time. Who knows what my friends have done to your friends? You guys have lost the very thing that is the most important to you: Invincibility. I may not have a fight with you , but when I'm dead and gone, you're going back to a world that knows how flawed you are and how a random person exposed that. You see Pilot, I accepted my fate days ago, but I just want to remind you that I'm going to die feeling victorious for what happened, and because I'll forever know, your reputation is broken because of me."

The Pilot kept moving, but he wasn't focused. In fact, he looked conflicted, as if he had something to say, but knew he couldn't say it. The Troll was playing a game he'd played many times on the boards: Offense. When others played defense, they were too busy defending themselves to pay attention to the accuser. The Troll had an advantage: A man who wouldn't defend himself with words would easily become frustrated, conflicted, make mistakes.

Anything to take The Pilot's attention off of his own footing would work just fine.

The Pilot tried to move faster forward than The Troll moved backward. Shadows crossed their faces as they pursued in a very slow chase. The Troll tried to pick up the pace, but realized his foot had been on the very edge of a beam. He shifted back to the center and began sliding his shoes back, as if moon-walking.

"Everyone else has these built in superpowers," The Troll said. "All they did was give you an airplane? What you guys do? Line up and proclaim what you wanted to be and everyone else had a talent except you? You just stared silently because you're too dumb to say anything intelligent and they said 'how about we just put him in a vehicle'? It's pathetic Pilot. It really is. What exactly makes you special? Wait...don't answer that," The Troll mocked. "Silence."

He realized The Pilot was really moving now, one foot expertly stepping over the other with both hands on the cable.

"You know the problem with silence though?" The Troll asked. "Everyone thinks you're a joke and you just have to take it up the tailpipe. And if you did talk, you'd make an even bigger fool of yourself. You don't have talent. You can't fly. You're not as strong as all the others. You Pilot, are a professional failure."

A window suddenly opened. The Pilot had closed enough distance and was a few feet away. The Troll could see the features on his face and the hardened jaw he was famous for. They stood on the same beam and held the same cable, and The Pilot was too focused on gaining on The Troll to see the whole picture.

The Troll suddenly yanked the cable toward them both with a sudden pull of the hands. He reached out and balanced himself immediately after, pressing his hand against another beam opposite the cable, but The Pilot didn't see it coming and suddenly was pulled backward with nothing to hold onto. He tried to grab the cable, but only managed to hook his index finger around it. The Troll shook it again, and suddenly The Pilot's body was in a moment of free-fall. The Pilot flailed wildly, catching onto the beam he'd previously been standing on at the last second with his fingers, his weight dangling below him and working against him. His sunglasses fell off his face and after a few moments, hit the water below.

The Troll stared down at The Pilot, who looked up at him with desperation in his eyes. He tried to reach his hand up, as if asking for a hand to pull him up.

"Use your words," The Troll said, taunting him.

The Pilot said nothing. He grabbed the beam again for leverage and reached his other hand up, moving his fingers desperately.

"I don't read sign language," The Troll said, and then pulled himself down into a sitting position and straddled the beam right above The Pilot. "Let's face it: You'd kill me. I can't pull you up."

The Pilot's eyes begged and finally, he managed words. "I don't...want...to die."

The Troll was almost sympathetic but something else came to him instead—something very real, and as he said it, his fingers typed it.

"I just wanted to be left alone. I didn't choose to do this. I was forced to pick the side I wasn't even on. And to top it all off, you still treated me like an enemy. You still acted like I was less than you. And even though I was on your side when this started, the only reason I'm not anymore, is because you forced me to be the opposing side. You forced me to fight back. You don't have the right to complain that your life is going to be ended by the same monster you created. I didn't kill you Pilot. You killed yourself."

Before either could say anything more, The Pilot let go and fell.

When The Troll found the pavement again, he squinted as he adjusted to the light. The sun was high enough in the sky now and everything was surprisingly quiet. He started his walk to the end of the bridge and to Heritage Square. It wasn't long before he realized something was wrong. At a distance, he could see Iris standing on the edge of the bridge looking back at...

The Poet?

That loser wasn't supposed to be here. He started walking faster, trying to register the situation. Iris looked on the verge of jumping, but paused when she saw The Troll coming at a distance.

The Poet turned his attention too and smiled upon seeing The Troll. "Draw near young knave," The Poet said. "I undergo a judicious journey to bring vengeance to you, you insolent mushroom."

The Troll stopped and frowned. "Um...I doeth not und'rstandeth how this works argal I will not useth it. Doeth though wanteth to shove a rotten hog up thy asshole?"

The Poet held Rainbow high, ready to toss it into the water. "Join her," he said, his smile gone.

"And do what? Jump? No way."

"Do it or this is gone forever."

"Good," The Troll said. "I love Psi. Always have. It's the tools who control it that are the joke."

"Your call," The Poet said and brought his hand back.

"Wait!" Iris shouted, desperately. The Poet paused as she turned to The Troll. "Please...don't do this."

"Don't do what?" The Troll asked. "He's the one doing it."

"Don't let him destroy it."

"He'll destroy it either way," The Troll said. "And even if he didn't, if we jump and die, there's no one left to use it anyway."

"Someone will someday," she said, tears forming in her eyes. "If it's destroyed, there will be nothing left that can shut Psi down."

"So what?" The Troll said with a shrug.

Her sadness turned to disdain. "You're an awful human being," she said, and though he pretended it didn't, it wounded him. "The Guide was right about you. Everyone was. I shouldn't have picked you. I don't know what I was thinking."

"You're asking me to die for something that can't be done and never will be. We will drown and he'll either destroy it or they'll lock it up. Best case scenario is they let another troll try to bring it across country and he wouldn't make it out of state either. There is no way that Psi will ever end, unless they decide to end it."

Iris turned to The Poet instead. "Please..." she said, begging him with her eyes.

"Please what?" The Poet asked. "Don't flatter yourself my delicate rose. I have no favors for you. You've wounded me where no man shall feel pain."

The Troll looked to Iris quizzically.

"I kneed him in the testicles," she said.

The Troll grimaced, but it disappeared a moment later.

"No jesting?" The Poet asked, studying The Troll's face.

"I honestly assumed you didn't have testicles," The Troll said.

"Your troll was right," The Poet said, facing Iris. "You never had a chance."

And then he threw it over the edge, so simply and quickly that it took half a minute to realize he'd really thrown it. "There," he said, and pulled a gun from the back of his pants. "I'm reminded of a sonnet..."

Then, to everyone's surprise, Rainbow flew back up over the edge, over The Poet's head, and landed in the middle of the street. If tensions weren't so high, it might have even been humorous, but in the moment, it only perplexed everyone. The realization that someone had to have thrown it took a long time to sink in, but when it did, The Poet turned and looked over the edge.

A second before, The Acrobat leaped from a beam at his side, grabbed a cable, swinging in an arc over and around The Poet, and just as The Poet realized something was happening, The Acrobat crashed into him, wrapping his arms around The Poet and letting the momentum of his motion send both of them off the bridge to the water below.

Everything was silent again and all that remained was The Troll, Iris, and Rainbow.

The Guide's world was moments away from ending, but he felt one last burst of energy within. The problem was that whatever that burst caused him to do, it would only buy him moments before two bounty hunters and five bots came down on him at once. What The Guide needed was for a burst of energy to be enough to eliminate everyone and everything in one shot.

He felt cold steel stuffed into his shoes, digging into his ankle, and remembered he still had a keepsake from his time in the jail. He'd used a pair of handcuffs to lock The Troll up. He'd kept a pair for himself.

The bots pushed him further into The Mortician's radius, but he frantically inventoried the placement of everything around him. He was a leap over the railing to the floor below. It would be a hard landing, but would buy him time before the bots could catch up. Above him was the pipe that ran to the faucet. If broken, water would cascade down, washing away the metallic gel. And if everything worked the way he'd played it in his head, that left The Coach—who would walk one floor down with one of his pouches and put a fresh coat on him immediately after.

He knew he had to move fast, but was interrupted by The Mortician, who grabbed his wrist and sent a surge of electricity up his arm. The Guide winced as his skin slowly started to rot, his veins turning blue and protruding from his skin as he felt the poison spread past his elbow and up his arm. He could control the rest of his body, but only until it reached his heart.

He let out a scream, partly from pain, but the true motivation was to initiate a burst of energy that only had to carry him for about thirty seconds.

The bots were moving away, letting The Mortician have his fun, and his window of opportunity had opened, but would close just as fast. He felt the pain shoot though his shoulder and reach his chest.

With his other arm, he reached down and brought his foot up, clinging onto the handcuffs with his fingers. He strengthened his grip and brought one end down over the pipe above him. The other, with some finagling, he clasped over The Mortician's wrist, causing The Mortician to loosen his grip. The Mortician was suddenly aware of his own predicament, his arm reaching out of the elevator cage, fastened to a pipe outside the cage. He tried to track what The Guide intended to do, but by the time he figured it out, there was no power to stop it.

The Guide let himself drop to the ground with all his weight, and suddenly, the cuffed hand of The Mortician was bound to the pipe above and unable to reach The Guide. The Mortician's other hand pulled back into the elevator, and he didn't bother with The Guide. Instead, he began to tug at the handcuffs, desperate to free himself without pushing any buttons that could result in ripping his hand off.

The Guide used every bit of momentum he had to send himself souring over the rails and to the platform below, landing on his feet and knocking the wind out of him as he crashed to the ground. He ignored the pain as he pushed himself back up and ran back to the elevator and hit the button with the arrow pointing down. A moment later, the elevator hummed to life and started moving to his floor.

The Coach's eyes went wide and he ran to help his friend, but as the elevator slowly went down, The Mortician found himself suspended in midair within the elevator, held in place by the handcuff while the elevator around him kept moving descending. The Mortician looked to his friend with desperation in his eyes. "Help!" he shouted. "Get it off me!"

The Coach only stared, frozen in place as he watched the situation helplessly. The elevator reached The Mortician's head, and suddenly was pushing his body down, while his arm pulled the opposite direction. Two things happened at once: The Mortician let out a terrifying scream as his body all at once disjointed and everything inside him shattered, and the pipe above him bent, sending a waterfall to the floor, which then seeped through the metal wiring, falling onto The Guide below.

He worked quickly, washing himself of all traces of the gel. The bots had already started the chase, but slowed as the gel mixed with water and fell to the ground below. Finally, they stopped, with nothing left to chase.

When it all became clear to The Coach that The Guide had beat the majority of them at once, he knew he had to act fast. He hurried down the stairs, reaching into his jacket and pulling another pouch. "You're going to pay for this!" he shouted, but his words only echoed in the factory. When he reached the third floor landing, there was no sign of The Guide. He walked slowly with the pouch in his upturned palm, ready to throw it on The Guide the moment he figured out where he was.

"You got nothing left Guide," he shouted. "You might as well give up."

He quickly turned a corner, expecting to see The Guide standing there, but moved slowly again upon seeing it was just another empty landing. At every corner was darkness. The Guide was tired and every moment wasted, he could be recovering, rebuilding his strength, and ready to strike.

Then he did from behind. He wrapped his arms around The Coach, but The Coach wasted no time to back him into the wall, smashing his body against the brick and sending him to the ground below. The Guide scurried away backward on his hands and feet, crab-walking quickly, but The Coach towered above him, gripping the pouch and holding it above him with a sadistic smile on his face. Before he could throw it, The Guide was on his feet, running toward him again, his arms wrapping around The Coach and trying to wrestle him down. The Coach brought an elbow down on his back and The Guide flattened face down on the platform again, rattling the ground. He slowly rolled to his back, wheezing, breathless.

He was done.

The Coach crouched down to one knee and leaned toward him. "I'm going to let my players kill you slowly, putting a thousand cuts on your body so you bleed out for days. You're going to wish you hadn't killed my friend. You're going to beg for anyone to come for you, but I'll be sitting right outside, waiting."

The Guide said something, but it came out as a whisper.

The Coach leaned in.

The Guide said it again, but barely had a breath left.

The Coach leaned in again, and suddenly The Guide's arm shot up, and the shattered glass The Acrobat had given him was stabbed into The Coach's shoulder, but not before going through the pouch first. Metallic gel oozed out onto The Coach, covering his skin and running over his wound, mixing with his blood.

"What?..." was all he could say before the bots began moving. The Guide fell back again and slowly pushed himself away from The Coach, whose eyes were darting back and forth, trying to make a decision between running and trying to finish off The Guide. He could control their speed to an extent, but he couldn't extinguish their hunger for the gel. "Get it off me!" he screamed, and suddenly looked back for where the pipe had been spraying water. It was now two stories up and only droplets fell. He knew he wouldn't make it back in time. Suddenly, he was surrounded by bots coming down on him. He tried to get away, but only managed to find the edge of the platform which in his desperation to escape, he toppled over backward. His body hit the railing below and nestled there for a moment before he slid off and fell to the first floor.

As The Guide slowly limped his way down the stairs and to the first floor, he passed The Coach on his way out, who only laid sprawled out on the ground with five bots surrounding his body and tearing it up.

The Guide tried to hurry to Iris, but couldn't find the strength. Instead, he dragged himself at the pace he was able, until he was back at the fountain. It was there that he first saw The Troll searching the area. Not far from The Troll, Iris was doing the same. She stopped as if sensing he was standing there and turned. Upon seeing him there, she ran to his arms and hugged him.

From where The Troll stood, he watched. He put his hand in his pocket and wrapped his fingers around Rainbow.

A mile downstream, The Poet got caught in a thicket of branches and weeds that protruded from the riverbank.

It was there that The Magician found him and hauled him to safety. He spit up a mouthful of water and stretched his body out on a large rock, letting the sun dry him off while The Magician stood over him and waited patiently.

When The Poet was ready, they walked through the sludge and over a bank of rocks until they were in a thicket of trees. The Poet glanced up for a moment and stopped at the site of The Acrobat, propped against a tree, having been saved moments earlier.

The Acrobat froze in place when he saw The Poet—the only man who knew his secret and The Poet was more than willing to spill.

"He threw me over!" he yelled, pointing his finger at The Acrobat accusingly. "I had Rainbow. They were all as good as dead. He threw me over!"

The Magician turned and studied The Acrobat's face, watching every movement.

"I admit that I was at fault," The Acrobat said, "But I wasn't trying to throw Poet over. I was trying to help and unfortunately, I got in the way."

"This is absurd!" The Poet yelled. "I know what took place!"

The Magician approached The Acrobat and studied his mannerisms, aware that The Acrobat tensed up, that his hairline had a line of sweat, that his eyes were widened and there was fear within. "Do you believe in Psi?" he asked.

"Of course I do."

"Are your loyalties with The Moderator?"

"Yes. Absolutely."

The Magician took another long moment to stare into his eyes until he finally smiled and put his arm around The Acrobat. "How about a little magic?"

The Acrobat nodded, but was tense under The Magician's touch.

The Magician took off his black hat and turned it in his hand, expertly spinning it with his index finger.

"Pick a card," he said.

The Acrobat hesitated. "I've seen this trick."

"Oh no," The Magician said. "You haven't seen *this* trick. Pick a card."

"Ace of spades," The Acrobat said.

The Magician took his hand off his back, having led him close to the riverbank. "Ace of spades," The Magician said, feigning a search for the card in the trees. "Pick a different card," he finally said.

"I think we need to regroup and…" was all The Acrobat could say before he was forced backward and thrown into the water. His head came above the surface for a moment, but was quickly forced back under. The Magician watched with a wide smile.

The Poet got to his feet, alarmed by his actions. "What are you doing?"

"My friend, we do not have the wiggle room for the kind of failure you've displayed today."

"We'll kill him," The Poet said quickly. "There's no doubt about it."

"Of course we will," The Magician said as The Acrobat tried to cling to something but only found air. "The whole world just saw them win a battle and at least one of our own is gone—maybe more. By the time the sun sets tonight, how will the world perceive us? We have been outwitted by a very small man and you were there Poet. You had him. Rest assured that if you cross paths again and The Troll walks away, I will saw you in half, and it won't be a trick."

The Acrobat weakened, and as his body stopped moving, Chameleon could be seen holding him down, her reflective surfaces catching sunlight, revealing her body.

The last thing The Acrobat saw before darkness overcame was the ace of spades.

CHAPTER 7

The Troll, Iris, and The Guide stood in the middle of the bridge looking out into the sky. They all digested the events of the day, in disbelief that it all went as planned. For the first time since they met, all tension was gone between The Troll and The Guide, but neither knew what to say to each other. They were opposite ends of the same coin, but somehow, The Guide had realized that The Troll could be the yin to his yang. They could compliment each others weaknesses. Maybe there really was room in the revolution for an antagonist. Sometimes, it was a worthwhile trait to just be able to piss people off.

"We're going to need to move," The Guide said, and they all nodded in agreement, but lingered a little longer so they could dwell on their victory before they went back to business as usual.

"What if The Acrobat is still alive?" The Troll asked.

"If he is, I doubt he'd want to come with us," The Guide said. "To the outside world, what we're doing is still impossible. When this is over, we'll make sure to make it right with him." He turned to The Troll, who looked sad that The Acrobat wouldn't be joining them. "What happened in that cell Troll?"

"Nothing," The Troll said. "We just spent a lot of time dying together, but I realized that The Acrobat wasn't loyal to The Moderator. I could just see it."

"The other bounty hunters won't be influenced in the same way,"

Iris said.

"I know," The Troll responded.

"I'm going to check the plane and see if there's a life raft in there," The Guide said. "We need to lose any evidence of a trail. We'll head down the river a couple days and head west from there." The Troll and Iris both nodded in agreement. "Will you be coming along?" The Guide asked, waiting for The Troll to answer.

If he wanted to, The Troll could go into hiding now and let them fulfill the mission, but he suspected once they were gone, he'd spend the rest of his life—however short that would be—regretting it. "I'll go if you don't mind."

The Guide nodded and wandered off toward the plane and began to dig through the wreckage.

Iris and The Troll stood silently for a long moment. "Why do you call yourself Iris?" The Troll finally asked.

"My mother loved flowers," she said, simply.

The Troll nodded. "You know, I still wish you hadn't picked me to do this. You basically killed me. I admire the revolution and I admire people who die for what they believe, but you shouldn't force people into that position."

"I know," she said. "I'm sorry. I just…I didn't have anyone else. I needed strong will."

"I don't have strong will. I'm just a guy who likes to get reactions."

"I think you do have strong will," she said, smiling and looking deep into his eyes. "You're just not angry enough yet."

"And how do I become angry?"

"When you see with clarity…when you see what a person really is and not just the person they want you to think they are…"

"Is The Moderator truly evil?" The Troll asked.

"Yes."

"He didn't seem evil."

"When you see that he is, it will change everything."

The Guide returned with a large piece of plastic rolled under his arms. He tossed it into the air and it suddenly inflated. By the time it landed, their life boat sat on the cement. "Only one thing left to do," The Guide said. "We need to transmit again. We need to tell everyone what happened here today. We need to recruit." He stared at The Troll.

"Not me. I'm not doing it."

"Why not?"

"Because I don't know what to tell people."

"Like it or not, you're the face of this now. I'm a soldier. People need to see that the one chosen is a leader who has followers."

The Troll turned to Iris, who stared at him, disappointed that he didn't have it in him. "I'm not ready yet," he said. "Maybe soon, but not yet."

The Guide left it at that, and walked a few feet away to set the transmitter up to broadcast his own face. He looked over his shoulder at The Troll as if giving him one last chance, but The Troll didn't move. The Guide flipped a switch.

The monitors flashed in the sky and suddenly The Guide had the floor. This time though, he shared it with The Moderator, who was seemingly waiting on the other end to intercept the transmission. The Moderator turned toward the screen and came face to face with The Guide, displeased to see him.

"Where are my men?" The Moderator asked, wasting no time.

"I have nothing to say to you," The Guide said and addressed the camera instead. "This goes out to the world…The men of Circular Prime do not have complete control. We've eliminated half of his bounty hunters in one day with a very small population. To those of you who do not have Psi, we need your…"

"You are breaking every law we have by broadcasting Guide!" The Moderator said, anger in his voice. His neck began twitching and he tried speaking, but couldn't get the words out.

"You made up every law you have," The Guide said. "We happen to disagree with your laws. You were going to kill millions of people because of the actions of one person. How do you justify that?"

The Moderator stared long and hard into the camera, aware that the world was watching and that this day belonged to The Guide. "What do you want Guide?" he asked.

"I want to talk to The Surfer. I want to see that he's okay."

"Bring him in," The Moderator shouted over his shoulder. They waited silently for five minutes, the screens only plastered with their faces. From the sidelines, The Troll and Iris watched the exchange with fascination, surprised at how much control they had over The Moderator. Finally, The Surfer was brought into the room. He looked haggard and tired and walked slowly as he found his circulation. The Moderator stepped out of the view of the camera as if to allow The Surfer and The Guide to have their moment.

The Surfer looked at The Guide confused, unaware of the morning's events.

"Surfer," The Guide said, a relieved smile filling his face. "You have no idea how good it is to…"

The moment ended as the screen filled with blood and The Surfer's eyes rolled back and he fell to the ground with a thud, a patch of his scalp hitting the wall behind him as he exited the screen. The Moderator filled the screen again, a smoking gun in his hand.

The Guide wanted to scream "no," but his voice caught in his throat and he began heaving and lost all sensation in his body. He tried to walk, but fell to his hands and knees as his limbs became rubber. He crawled to the edge of the bridge, his forehead resting against a beam. Iris hurried to his side and held his shaking body. She held him close and turned back to the screen where behind the splatter of blood, The Moderator sat patiently waiting with a smug smile on his face.

"Turn it off!" Iris screamed and The Troll's eyes went wide and he hurried toward the transmitter, suddenly with his face on the screen. He reached for the switch.

"Troll…" The Moderator said. "My offer is still good." The Troll paused and stared at The Moderator, who suddenly looked innocent and sincere. "I can have someone there within half an hour. You've been through a lot. You have a home here. Aren't you tired of this game?"

The words echoed in The Troll's head as he considered what The Moderator was saying. He thought about the events that led him here: Who he once was, who he still believed himself to be, of Wigeon, The Surfer, the bounty hunter dinner, The Acrobat….The Guide…Iris…"

"You've got to be tired of this game," The Moderator said again, compassion in his voice.

"Yeah," The Troll said, dryly. "I am."

The Moderator smiled, pleased to hear this. Everything that happened flashed through The Troll's head with one final sentiment:

You're not angry enough yet. And then he understood what Iris and The Guide were all about. There were some things in the world that you just couldn't bend to, no matter how much power they held.

"I *am* tired of this game," The Troll said again, still in a state of shock, and then began speaking slowly, his fingers speaking the words with him. "So we're going to change it…"

The smile faded from The Moderator's face.

"…We're going to hunt your guys now," The Troll said, his eyes moving back and forth rapidly as he found his words. His fingers began shadow-typing faster and his eyes found the camera as if he were staring directly at The Moderator. "We killed half of your friends today. I'm sure it's hard for you Moderator. I'm sure it's hard for you to sit there and try to give off the impression that you're flawless while you're really angry inside that you're guys are dead at our hands. I had such a good day. I could make a list of great things that happened today. I crashed The Pilot's plane. I killed The Pilot after he begged for his life. The Poet got kicked in the nads…

You know, you don't have a very large population in Chicago. Your group is small because you trust them…they're your closest friends. It must hurt knowing we killed them Moderator. How much love did you have for your Coach and your Mortician and Pilot, and for Acrobat and that awful Poet? How much does it hurt that three people eliminated them within minutes?"

The Moderator tried to hold his composure, but his neck twitched and his face warped into something that looked like pain mixed with hatred.

"You wouldn't have accepted me into Chicago Mod. You propositioned me in secret to betray those who are against Psi. You told me to transmit and destroy Rainbow and you did it to give off an appearance, because the rest of the world are hostages…puppets because they carry Psi…because if they speak out, you simply deactivate them. You boast about how the world is peaceful now, but it's not. It's just controlled. They stay quiet out of fear. I can't recruit them to join us because you'll just kill them, and so we'll just take care of this ourselves. But you propositioned me. Why? Because you know you're wrong. Because you need to keep your evil hidden by pretending the world loves you, when they actually fear you, or in my case, just think you're a giant tool.

You know, I really enjoyed killing your Pilot. Partly because he was such an asshole and partly because he was your friend. I look forward to meeting the rest of your friends and killing them too. I really hope they find us fast because I think I can be good at ruining them. When I do, I'll get a nice close-up shot for everyone to see."

Everyone watched closely from living rooms around the world, from in their yards or their local pubs. The Gambler and The Weatherman halted their journey to watch, The Poet stirred inside as The Troll's face filled the sky. The Mentalist studied his face from his suite in Vegas, hoping he would make the journey so he could put an end to his boasting. Behind him, Wigeon's face was glued to the screen. The Chameleon and The Magician watched expressionless, plotting their attack, and The Moderator tightened his fists off camera, speechless, but stewing.

Ten feet from The Troll's side, Iris looked up and watched wide-eyed, and The Guide wiped away tears and watched silently, pushing all emotion aside and admiring the face of the revolution as he trolled with his anger finally in the right place.

"We'll find them and kill them, and why stop there? We don't need to go to Vegas to shut you down. We don't carry Psi. We'll just come straight back to Chicago to ruin everything you've built. I'll burn your city to the ground and when you come running out, we'll take you down too.

You made a mistake when you took Psi out of me Mod. You made a mistake when you left your family to die along with millions of people when you turned Psi on the population. I'm sure the ghost of your wife and daughter are sitting with you now, ashamed of what an ass-hat of a person you turned out to be and hawking spirit-spit on your ugly twitchy face. You once justified your actions by saying: when gods fight, they step on ants, but you're flattering yourself way too much, you narcissistic piece of shit. You're nothing more than a four year old with a magnifying glass, burning ants because you're emotionally immature and in need of attention. Oh, you got fired from your job. Boohoo. How horrible. Try being one of the many people you murdered or their family left behind that have to mourn them and then whine about your dumb problems. You brag about bringing peace, as if anyone could ever believe that a mass murderer has a conscience."

"Are you done yet?" The Moderator started to say. "Because…"

"You'll know I'm done when I stop talking and when I stop

talking, I'm shutting down the broadcast because I can't think of anything in this world that I care less about than whatever bullshit you're going to fire off when I finish.

You lost today Mod and you lost big, and the world saw it, and to the world: Soon, you will no longer be enslaved by Psi. This moron has been in charge way longer than he should have been. Just hang tight. You'll know you're free when you see The Moderator paraded around town with his head on a stick."

The Moderator opened his mouth, but The Troll shut down the broadcast. Moments later, the screens turned on and The Moderator broadcast more of the same: "Follow the rules...the rebels are terrorists...I created peace," but it didn't sound the same. It sounded phony and transparent, and even The Moderator had lost his showmanship.

The Troll grabbed the life boat and brought it to the edge of the bridge and turned to The Guide, who hadn't recovered, but looked hopeful after The Troll's trolling. "We ready to do this?" he asked.

"I thought you said we were going back to Chicago," Iris said.

"Strategic thinking," The Troll said, tapping his temple. "Give them another direction to watch. We can get this thing to Vegas. I learned a little about the layout of the land from The Acrobat. There are ways to get there. We just have to find them." He reached out and extended his hand to The Guide, who slowly reached up and let The Troll hoist him to his feet. "The Surfer was a good man," The Troll said. "Let's finish what he started."

The Guide said nothing. He walked ahead and The Troll and Iris followed as they descended the hill and climbed into the life boat. As the current took them down the river far from the bridge, Iris and The Guide fell asleep in each others arms. The Troll watched them, wishing it was him instead. He watched as the scenery passed, wondering if he had what it took to fulfill this mission, but knowing he would at least make life as hard as possible and do as much damage as he could along the way.

I'm a Troll, he thought. *And I'm the face of a revolution.* He laughed to himself as he shook his head in disbelief. It wasn't the best combination of things to be, but maybe it was exactly what the world needed.

A note about trolling from the Author

A little over fifteen years ago, I decided I would try my hand at screenwriting. I wrote what I believed to be the best script ever written at the time, though to this day, I have a hard copy in a binder that I refuse to open because I know I'll cringe at how bad it really is. The script led to the next which led to nine scripts, all of which will never see the light of day, but through screenwriting, I became a troll, and eventually, a writer.

Let's go back in time a bit. Fifteen years ago, I had what I believed to be a great script. I knew nothing about what I was supposed to do with it, so when a friend told me about a reality series called Project Greenlight, the brain-child of Ben Affleck and Matt Damon, which was essentially a scriptwriting contest, I submitted immediately. Those who entered a script were to read at least three other scripts entered, judge them, and the thousands of scripts entered would filter down to 250. They would be filtered two more times until only one winner remained and that script would be made into a movie.

For those of you wondering, I didn't make the first cut. I entered all three years that Project Greenlight existed and never made the first cut. Each time, I thought I had gold. Each time, my ego took a hit. I don't write screenplays anymore and I have no desire to, but Project Greenlight was a gigantic spark in my life that set me on a path that ultimately led me here. Without it, I would have moved in another direction and I have no idea what I would be doing today.

Project Greenlight had a message board. I can still remember the green font and black background of the boards. I remember going there because I was navigating the site to expand my knowledge of all things screenwriting.

When I found a board where hundreds of users were discussing writing, arguing with each other, critiquing each others work, I knew it was something I needed to pay attention to. I lived in a small-town in Iowa and never interacted with people who shared my passion and here I'd fallen into a crowd of witty, intelligent people who knew something about writing. I latched on to some and others I ignored, but for awhile, I read what they had to say and learned what I could. To my surprise, there were relationships, rivalries, and group discussions. It resembled, believe it or not, a community.

Then one day, under the user-name mcbrainder, I jumped into a thread and posted.

I don't remember what the fight was about. It was two users, arguing back and forth. I thought I had something witty to say and attacked one of them with what I believed was a clever comeback. A moment later, two other users attacked me back and told me that the user I attacked was a "good egg." Apparently I went after a popular user and picked the wrong side.

I don't remember the progression from there. I remember posting a lot, starting to fit in, making a name others knew, and somehow becoming part of an on-line community. I was still very young and playful. I didn't have contributions that would help an amateur learn the craft. Instead, I played the role of a goofball, and when I was tired of that, I started creating multiple user-names and posting as many people at once. At one point in time, I had as many as thirty user-names.

I'm aware of the fact that anyone reading this will have discovered that I had way too much time on my hands, and they'd be right. I got sucked into the message board vortex. If I'd spent that energy writing scripts, I probably would have produced ten times what I actually wrote. Instead, I interacted, and sometimes, I played the bad guy. Sometimes, I antagonized newbies just for sport.

Somewhere along the way, playful became mean and sport became Internet-vigilantism. As I became more intelligent, I would approach a conflicting viewpoint with a rant that I would use one of my fake names to voice. Mcbrainder remained a nice goofball, but I started to feel like I had something to say. I would see what I considered to be ridiculous behavior, attention seeking people in need of ego-boosts, and other users enabling them, telling them they were right (though often they were clearly self-destructive) and that it wasn't their fault. I wasn't a fan of victim mentality.

Enter me, trolling with my fake names, trying to hold a mirror up to people. Sometimes it was mean-spirited. Sometimes it was just brutal honesty, but brutal honesty that I knew would provoke attacks. I preferred to keep the attacks aimed at the names who weren't linked to my core name. As life progressed, I realized people had a lot to say to my fake names. Mcbrainder was just a goof who would get an "lol" here and there, but there was no substance behind that. People wanted to talk to the trolls, even if it's a negative experience. The common anti-troll stance is to say "Don't feed the trolls" because if you don't react to what they say, they go away, but the funny thing is, people feed trolls far more than they do serious posters.

I no longer troll, but if you visit any message board anywhere with high traffic, you will see that there are going to be a lot of threads clearly designed to antagonize, and many where someone has something they just want to say.

The threads where someone just wants to hold a discussion die. The trolls are fed constantly, and in saying "don't feed the trolls," they continually feed the trolls, because trolls only do what they do because everyone wants attention, and when a person can't find a positive way to create interest, they search for a negative way. Responses fuel trolling, and unless a thread sinks, every person in it has "fed the troll".

Contrast this with everything in life: The actress who thought her career would never take off and committed suicide by leaping from the Hollywood sign, kids who aren't acknowledged in positive ways and act out in negative ways because they know it's the way they'll be noticed, the man whose spouse cheats on him and he realizes his real self isn't good enough and offs himself and her. Everyone wants to be noticed, and when they're not noticed positively, they don't give up there. They find another way, often in ways that hurt other people or themselves.

It took me a long time to realize that trolling was just a waste of time, but so was being mcbrainder. Though Project Greenlight and those message-boards set me on a great path in life, I can look back now and I know that everything I did, good or bad, was to be noticed and I put too much energy into that—time I could have used creating other good things. Talking about what I was going to do took away so much time just doing what I needed to do. I have no regrets, but I could never troll again. It's simply something I did and snapped out of after awhile.

I've angered people in chat rooms. I once went to a role-play sex room and made someone cyber with me as The Hamburgler and him as The Pillsbury Dough Boy. I've been kicked off and banned from a Scientology board forever after multiple warnings from their moderators to stop pretending to be Xenu (I claimed I was the dictator of the Galactic Confederacy and my profile pics were of Alf). I once had a Kevin Federline Myspace page and interacted with his fans and even Brittany Spears, going out of my way to make him seem like a fool. I've had people threaten my life through Craigslist, and I've had people try to send me viruses.

Everywhere you go on-line, from the user comments on CNN to the IMDB message-boards, the majority of what you will see is vile, politically or religiously motivated, hatred. From fights between whether or not a movie was any good, to Facebook disagreements where friends become enemies because of their polar opposite viewpoints. People have become detached from one another because we see words—not faces. We can easily hide behind a keyboard, angry that life hasn't given us everything we want and channel that anger into spreading our poison to others.

Behind every user who is doing this, is a person who very likely is polite to their peers, loved by their friends, who spends holidays with their families and is maybe highly reputed at their job. No troll carries that troll persona throughout their daily life when they're off-line.

When I started writing The Troll, my hero was not a troll, but as the idea developed, I came across the anti-troll creed on an article: Don't feed the trolls," followed by, "He's probably just some kid in the safety of his parent's basement. He wouldn't say this if he was face to face with us. He's a coward."

No truer words could be typed. Most trolls are likely decent people. Put them behind a keyboard, and a beast is unleashed. Put them in a room full of strangers, they probably try to fit in. People aren't truly trolls in life. People are just people who turn into trolls when they sit behind a screen and forget that a user-name represents an actual person. It makes them a coward, but not necessarily a bad human being.

The stage was set: A world where no one could speak out against authority because to do so could mean instant death. I knew my hero had to be a troll. There was no better demonstration of my feelings on Internet bullying versus living among people in real life.

Maybe the problem is we're too dependent on electronics. Maybe the problem is that people need to be reminded that other people essentially all want the same things to be happy. Maybe there's no problem at all and we need to brush off the words of strangers.

I hope this story is something everyone can relate to in some small way. We all pick our battles carefully and we all know when to shut up or speak up, but whether you're the troll, or the person being trolled, at the end of the day, whether you take route A, B, or C, for most of us, the destination is the same.

Thank you for reading part one of The Troll.

I encourage you to leave a review of my book at: TheTroll

https://www.amazon.com/review/create-review? ie=UTF8&asin=1511407204&channel=detail- glance&nodeID=283155&ref_=cm_cr_dp_no_rvw_e&store=b ooks#

Please, no reviews from Scientologists.

Special Thanks

Beta readers:
Sunshine Yoders, Jennifer Darr, Michael La Ronn, Joey Dursky.

Acknowledgments

Special thanks to usernames who were more than just usernames to me:

The Dread Pirate Morgan, Redwings16, khleigho, Amil, MagicallyDeelicious, Amj, Uilani, Dirt, Aurora2001, saeph47, Aspie, Grimaceb, GeoffFoley

Other cool people, many of whom I haven't met:

Stonygirl, bonadea, mets, Beaver Toast, felix black, Devereaux, Chereefrog, alexus, vorpal, Sam, edgewyze, BillytheKid, JackAwful, CDNFilm, PearlsBeforeSwine, frederickcleveland, Jack's Wasted Life, Jack's Wasted Liver, RandallFlagg, Quetee, Queen Uhuru, Queenie, Nostromo, Rockstar, Dr. Gonzo, Red Rover, summer, mack daddy, oliver, daisy, maze, walt, stacy, MingChen, bjn, quickkick, Daisyphreak, RickDeckard, justina, Naseer, Couchguy, Dfogg, backgroundgrrl, Smichael, petunya, Safteydancer, Hong Kong Cavaliers, Shine, outsiders, eyesnot, magicalcat, DLane, Siren Six, skeely, hikarate, Tyson Zoltan, Heder, El Topo, Steel Linx, mdb, coyotesix, gnasche, not that button!, Misterorange, markpenny, celticjack, 1take, Wrighty8, Motherof8, atezinc, Pinata, heizer, Shapely Stooge, Talespinner, Mihalow, patthedog, Siren Six, Estrogen, Mjarbo, Hollygolightly72, Rollerfink, Webster, ToeJam, Abbe, flikwrtr, OscarETTE, Skeeley, noonespecial2310, Joe's Hero, scribbler, Gamma, SirVince, dawncallahan, pinto, carv, KSoze327, Meskey, dawncallahan, Ajl, FilmAsArt, Hassamassahoff, Jeskey, dafemmefatale, marcn, Jennifer8, Mojave, Keesha63, tombliss, mrshakopter, Stacy,

Bittrich, HarmonieMoore, tpow, maestro8, Grimlock,
TeresaMLA, Complexman, Eddie Zipperer, krowkcolcfilms, Stone
Rose, bunny, Fivepointfilms, beazyb, Hammered, mjfryar, Aryss,
Jp, JusticePeace, Parrot, FutureMrsAffleck, FutureMrsDamon,
darzam, Rocketman, Izzy, Nephratari, drenajo, Shilohswolf,
fiveswinya, closetwriter, celticjack, Sallyomally, 1take, smichael,
Legendmaker, Keesha63, Americano, Ksoze327, Gnasche,
JovianDeadees, Furstlady, little devil, serendipity, not that button!,
meskey, RickDeckard, Artra, Toejam, Wasabi, Bigfish, Oscarette,
Jefferson, Carv, Limpsquiggy, Sam Raimi, snack daddy,
pinorpala, makememeow, Blue Cardinal, backgroundgrrl, Bruce,
Talespinner, Vance, Isabel, BigZWillis, gman8343, atezinc,
Hbeachbabe, dommah, abbe, Hippiechick, Wrighty8,
DeadlyBlackNinja, ANNOYANCE, CheezUMS, PartyofOne,
AsRiaL, Bad David, Andromeda, typo, Webster, lax211, Athanor,
Gwinks18, Maven Quibble, cloudkick, Hawking, lostfairytales,
theblondewritr, frederickcleveland, Batgirl3780, IcequeenJ,
meow, vanilla thunder, Trufaut Cavalier, Damian, A true faux
cavalier, Serenity7911, Pinky d elephant, Mojave,
CrackHeadKitty, 12vob, Whoopie Cushion, cw!, Wisened, julie,
vanderwoude, the apocalypse is upon us, Moria1, Chow,
Montanagrizgirl, Ilovemydogbutnotinthatway, Pickel87, Frosty,
1000$ per citizen, Ashlane, 2cute, Theodore Rex, Lkulikoff,
Hoaxed Totem, Gravity, Cbas, Salty I liftus, Juan Valdez,
Shankroid, Prettygurl, Poop club, The Marlboro Man,
ANNOYANCE., FilmAsArt, Str8jive, If hair was liquid I'd be Don
Johnson. For Real, Greendaze, strangerthanthou, dhh hhd, Bboog,
Bad juju, ms. spacecase, Hourly wages, Molly49, dmburrows,
Carrie, gldnswife, infinite monkeys, Karma Marie,
Sweetmellymel, smee, Mike Brady, Lilthblue, athenablue, Just
Reading N Stuff, Down and Out in NYC, dh!, 2questionable,
Actor director supreme, Actor burrito supreme, Beaker, jkk, Penny
Lane, DEVELOPEXEC, Miss lady Laura, Sassy, Fgonello,
paperstreet, Dijonete, Camirox, Whore of Mensa, Randall Flagg,
zackfu, plumsmuggler, Motley Cool, Disney69, athena, yeddle,
moviecre8r, dharris, Opie32, Kit, allyn, chinle, Bones, urnvs,
Mikeinlalaland, VLBarnhill, whosurdaddy, BigButtBlonde,
justcallmesandea, Shecky the goat boy, Urban Windingo, Texas
Dave, greggg, greenie, skuhn, hat, cafechick, tiny fonts,

Gracilou, Str8jive, scarlet begonias, Jade15, Shine, Enigmatic Flounder, otis the good time party clown, lilpixie, psychic, psychicmuse, animaxitele, Bruce, Grey, Captain Caveman, Seestone, KilgoreATrout, Cj220, longerfellow

Made in the USA
Lexington, KY
12 June 2015